MW01043228

THE SEARCH FOR THE
GREAT KIWI YARN

THE SEARCH FOR THE
GREAT KIWI YARN

Edited by Martin Crump

HarperCollins *Publishers*

National Library of New Zealand Cataloguing-in-Publication Data

The search for the great kiwi yarn / edited by Martin Crump.
ISBN 978-1-86950-657-5 (pbk.)
1. Folklore—New Zealand. 2. New Zealand wit and humor.
I. Crump, Martin, 1959-
398.20993—dc 22

First published 2007
HarperCollins*Publishers (New Zealand) Limited*
P.O. Box 1, Auckland

ISBN-13: 978 1 86950 657 5
ISBN-10: 1 86950 657 X

Cover design by Matt Stanton, HarperCollins Design Studio
Cover photo by Patrick Bellett Photography
Cover artwork by Jason Chatfield
Internal text design and typesetting by Janine Brougham
Printed by Griffin Press, Australia
79gsm Bulky Paperback used by HarperCollinsPublishers is a natural,
recyclable product made from wood grown in a combination of
sustainable plantation and regrowth forests. It also contains up to a
20% portion of recycled fibre. The manufacturing processes conform to
the environmental regulations in Tasmania, the place of manufacture.

Contents

Foreword

It's been just over eleven years since the death of one of the great yarn spinners and storytellers of our time, my father Barry Crump. The last thing I want to do is try to fill those shoes, but I believe it's important to record and capture those stories before they're lost. In this Internet age, we glance over stories lightly and discard them, so to have these gems in the tangible form of a book to reread and put a smile on our faces or even raise a laugh can only be a good thing.

A good yarn usually has a thin line of truth to it; the rest is in the telling. The more you tell it, the better shape it takes. You can make a yarn out of a joke, include a family member or friend in the starring role and expand it to end up with a yarn like this:

A guy (your friend or family member) goes to the doctor and says, 'I've got a problem but you must promise not to laugh.' The doctor says, 'Of course not, just show me.' Well, he drops his pants and there's the smallest willy you've ever seen. The doctor howls with laughter, and with tears rolling down his face he gets up off the floor, finally pulls himself together and says, 'Sorry, what seems to be the problem?' Your friend replies, 'It's swollen.'

With our attention spans shrinking by the minute,

if you can hold centre stage with a yarn and capture people's attention for a few minutes, you're doing your bit to keep this dying art alive. In this ridiculously PC world we're fast losing the ability to laugh at ourselves, which is another reason I chose to be involved with this book.

I hope this book inspires you to write, record or just keep retelling the yarns of your past. Capturing an atmosphere and a time on a page is a real talent and you'll never know if you can until you try. I've hung around enough with authors to know that if you get stuck, go back to your own experiences and you'll find things start to move again.

As for the telling of a yarn, there is an art to it — we've all been mesmerised by a good storyteller and we've all been bored by a bad one. Capturing your audience is first of all a matter of timing — the stage must be clear of distractions and when you start, get to the point. Don't fill your yarn up with details or you'll lose them. A laugh early on will help you hold their attention. The yarn must flow well, like all good stories, until everybody is hanging on your every word waiting for the twist at the end or an excellent punch line. If you manage this, you've probably got them for the evening and you've become an entertainer.

Good yarn spinners practise their yarns — family and friends are perfect to practise on before you start telling them to strangers. There is one great fear to overcome — the fear of no one laughing. I've been through it and probably will again. They say it's while you're dying that you're actually never more alive, and in a strange way I understand this. I can't promise it won't happen to you but if you're well prepared you'll minimise the risk. Confidence is the trick of not worrying about who is watching and listening to you, confidence in the yarn you know is funny and interesting. The rest is in your delivery.

The beauty of a book of yarns is that you can read a few, put it down and pick it up again whenever it suits. I hope you steal a yarn or two out of the book and retell them as your own, because where do you think we got them from? In this mad mixed-up world where we don't even know who our enemies are, I know one thing for sure: we could all use a good laugh.

Warmest regards
Martin Crump

Yarns

Uncle Hec

Martin Crump

Uncle Hec was a pretty smart businessman. He worked hard, wheeling and dealing and looking for profit wherever he could.

He promised himself that as a mark to show that he had made it, he would buy himself a new Mercedes. As he reached his 45th birthday he knew that the time had come and as he knew a man who knew a man, Uncle Hec got a good deal on a black, brand new 500SEL Mercedes. It was his pride and joy — gleaming, it was. Hec was out there with a rag cleaning the already shining, shark-like Mercedes like a man possessed.

When he was ready, he invited his wife Merle and the three children to come for a drive. First though, there were strict instructions not to touch anything — certainly there was to be no eating and if possible everyone was to keep their breathing to a minimum.

Everything was going well as they made their way out to the country. The family was starting to relax until they saw a sign saying *Lion Safari Park* and the kids started to yell: 'Can we, Dad, huh Dad, please Dad, can we please, please, c'mon, Dad!'

Merle gave her look to Hec. He pulled a face, squirmed a bit, muttered under his breath and finally gave in — turning the Mercedes into the entrance of the Lion Safari Park. The deal at the park was to pay for your ticket, buy some bags of food for the animals you could hand-feed, stay in the car at all times and follow the signs.

The lions were docile and lying about all over each other swotting the flies away with their tails, so not much action was happening there. The rhino, yes one rhino, was so far away you needed binoculars to see it — so not much action there either. Next they came to the enclosure that housed the donkeys, a couple of giraffes and the camels. These were all animals you could feed by winding down the window and holding out your hand heaped with food so they could come up and graze.

Action at last. Things started to get a little scary when an eager gathering clustered around the Mercedes and an excited and cheeky camel put his head through the back window to try to get at the middle child's bag of feed. This terrified the child by the window who pushed the electric window button hoping that the camel would pull out its head — but I'm afraid that instead it trapped the camel's head, terrifying the beast which started snorting, honking snot and saliva all over the children and the interior of the new Mercedes.

That was on the inside. Outside the car the camel was kicking the door panels with its hooves as the kids screamed in fear. Merle was screaming. Hec was screaming. A ranger ran over and rescued the camel. Hec and his family left the park but there was a silence and the feeling of a storm brewing all the way home. Without a word Merle and the kids trooped into the house, but Hec drove off to the RSA to console himself and check out the damage. Two of the door panels were a write-off, the wing mirror had gone, a tear had appeared in the upholstery and the interior needed a thorough clean.

Nearly in tears Hec went in for a beer and stayed for a few more as he recounted the day's events to his mates. When he had cooled down sufficiently to face the family, Hec headed home. As he drove away from the RSA, just a few hundred yards down the road he was pulled over by a cop who slowly walked around the Mercedes peering at all the dents, bumps and scratches. Finally, he looked questioningly at Hec for an explanation.

'A camel did it,' said Hec. Before he knew it he was blowing into the bag and as luck would have it he was just over the limit. Hec drives a Toyota now and nobody has mentioned his 45th birthday, the safari park, the Mercedes nor Hec's drink-driving conviction to this day.

Flora and the Bibles

Dianne Haworth

When the daughter of a prominent Auckland family, Flora McKenzie, took on a colourful career as one of New Zealand's most notorious 'madams', it was only a matter of time before she would run foul of the law.

For years a blind eye had been turned towards the goings-on at 'Flora's place' at 17–19 Ring Terrace in

Ponsonby, which attracted a clientele that cut across all barriers (it was reputed that a couple of the country's leading judges were seen leaving the place on more than one occasion). Her revolving waterbed on the top floor — with its panoramic views across St Marys Bay and Freemans Bay — was a particular attraction. However, following too many official complaints to be ignored, action had to be taken.

In July 1964 Flora was charged with keeping premises as a brothel and landed six months inside, followed by a year's probation. A couple of years later, in 1966, she was similarly charged and similarly convicted and, on being released, Flora once more returned to her home and her profession.

In late 1967 the police set a trap for Flora. An undercover policeman arrived at Ring Terrace with some marked notes for payment and said he was looking for a bit of 'slap and tickle'. However, before one of Flora's girls could oblige the prospective client, the place was raided by the police.

So Flora was back in court for the third time. Charged by the presiding judge, the jury and counsel visited Ring Terrace during the trial where they were flummoxed to be shown through the premises by plainly dressed women who wore no make-up. On each bed there sat a Bible, and a poster 'Jesus Saves' was on the noticeboard in the lounge, alongside a large cross and a Billy Graham pamphlet urging people to come to a crusade for the Lord.

Unable to agree whether Flora McKenzie was a misunderstood woman or a crafty madam, the jury was hung on both the first and second trials of 1967 and 1968. On 3 December 1968, the Crown flagged the case with the words 'proceedings stayed'.

And so Flora with her revolving bed at the top — where a good-looking young electrician who called in to fix it had so pleased Flora that he was invited 'to have a free one on the house' — and a coffin downstairs in the lounge, kept in case one of her clients died on the job, was left in peace for the remainder of her days.

In 1981 Flora was invited to contribute to the Ponsonby Personality Cookbook where she shared one of her favourite recipes with readers. It was for Whisky and Milk. 'Pour a glass of milk and add some whisky to it according to taste. Don't drink more than five glasses at a time,' she wrote, with the postscript, 'I gave up eating a long time ago.'

A true story?

Did you hear about the burglar who tried to break into someone's house using a credit card? Unfortunately the credit card broke off in the doorway. The homeowner gave the details to the police, who were easily able to trace the owner of the card. When the investigating policeman went to the card owner's house, they found the other half of the card sitting on the kitchen table. The burglar had used his own card, not even a stolen one!

Talkback

Martin Crump

I was very fortunate to be let loose on talkback radio, because at the time I knew nothing about it.

On my first night I was set to do a two-hour stint with Jim Sutton at Newstalk ZB, from 3 a.m. to 5 a.m. I got there early at 1 a.m. to watch before I went on. Jim was his own producer — answering callers while at the same time talking to others on-air. He was a good smooth operator.

I hadn't brought in any news topics with me — I would be flying by the seat of my pants and I was very nervous. When two o'clock rolled around with another hour still to wait, I asked Jim to stick me on as I couldn't stand the butterflies any more and I would do a runner if he made me wait any longer!

With Jim pushing the buttons for me, on I went — all I had to do was turn the mike on and talk. Well, talk I did for twenty-five minutes without a call, and I was beginning to die on air! I had been following Jim's subject but it wasn't getting the calls when a caller came in at last and off I went from that, for the three hours up until 5 a.m.! It was exhilarating — I could talk, but I still knew nothing about the job.

The boss called me in during the week and confirmed that I was useless but I could engage in conversation which was a strong requirement for overnight talkback. He gave me another opportunity, this time on my own for the full six-hour shift. With only six months' high-school education and no technical skills, I was a Luddite, so I brought in a buddy with me — Bryce Peterson, my old man's friend and producer from when Barry had had a show on Radio Pacific.

Nervous doesn't come close to how I felt; I was ill-prepared and it showed. I couldn't figure out how to take the station out of delay just before the news. Pressing this button, then that one was too much to remember for this lump. What a struggle it was until 3 a.m. when Bryce tried to ease the tension.

On the weekends the host read the news, sport and the weather. I was reading the sport about a Czech-oslovakian hammer thrower whose name I could not pronounce. He had made a crooked throw and killed an official on the sideline. On top of that — you know when you get the feeling someone is watching you — well, I looked up when I was reading and saw Bryce was standing naked at the studio window with his arse pressed against the glass.

That was it for me. Right in the middle of my read I burst out laughing and just managed to get through the weather. I must say, though, I was more relaxed for the rest of the show!

Periodically, I was given a night to cover for some-one . . . One night I was paying no attention to the caller and playing with the buttons. Do you know, I shut the whole station down — and twenty-three other frequencies around the country! I felt sick, sad, I just wanted to go home to Mother!

I rang another host and live on air at 2.30 a.m.

asked her what to do, but she couldn't help. I rang our technician — once again live on air — and he told me I had gone years back on the computer. He would have to come in to help me.

Despite these setbacks I was invited by the management to continue, even though Bryce and I knew nothing about ZB and its people. We were battling along one morning and at about 2 a.m. we saw somebody going in the back of the building. Bryce said he'd go and investigate. The intruder had his back turned so Bryce said, 'Oi, are you the cleaner?' Leighton Smith turned around and said, 'No, I'm not the cleaner.' He had just jumped off a plane and had come to check his mail!

At 5.15 a.m. another morning, as Paul Holmes' crew and production team were getting ready for Paul's number-one breakfast show, I was talking to someone whose voice was a warm monotone and I fell asleep! I woke up to silence and thought, 'I'm on air — but I was talking to somebody — have they hung up? — how long has there been silence?' so I said, 'Thank you for your comments there.' And I heard an answer! 'No trouble.' So I moved on — it was the silence that had woken me.

It's now ten years since I started, and I think I've improved a bit. It's live, it's instant and I love my job. I still make mistakes and have plenty to learn. Here's to the next ten years.

The call of the wild

Martin Kessick

The kakapo is a unique New Zealand treasure. An oversized, flightless, nocturnal parrot which stores energy as body fat, freezes when it is in danger and, despite its best efforts, doesn't breed every year. It's just a feathered version of your typical Kiwi bloke. But unlike the New Zealand male there are only eighty-six of these birds in existence. Each kakapo has a name and is listed internationally as a critically endangered species. And I'll tell you why . . .

In the 1990s the kakapo was on the verge of extinction. A sanctuary was established on Whenua Ho (Codfish Island), a bushclad island barely 3 km from the wildest stretch of the west coast of Stewart Island. It was here that a film crew planned to document the kakapo's plight, and they chose Lionel to do it.

Lionel was found on Stewart Island in 1981 and was moved to Whenua Ho to help perpetuate the species. The crew would follow Lionel for ten days towards the end of the four-month mating cycle and film him engaging with one of the sophisticated female kakapo on the island. On the first evening the crew followed Lionel on his 'lek', the mating system used by kakapo whereby the males enter into mortal combat for 'calling posts', specially dug-out bowls in the ground from which they 'call' every night. This 'call' reverberates through the cold night air on its 5 km journey to any willing female kakapo ear.

The trouble was, the ladies weren't listening. For the first three evenings Lionel walked and boomed and walked and boomed and walked and boomed. The crew walked and carried their boom, camera and lights. They got plenty of good 'lekking' footage, but no 'necking' footage! Sadly, Lionel could not pull.

Something was different about night number four. Although it was horrendous weather Lionel set out with a bright glint in his eye, a spring in his boom and his beak at a jaunty angle. He was an owl-faced, moss-coloured ladykiller that night and nothing was going to stand in his way. So when a mollymawk (a black-backed albatross) landed in front of Lionel, the feathers did fly. Lionel eventually emerged triumphant, the unfortunate mollymawk dead in his talons. All was caught on camera, the crew beside itself with excitement. Having proved his masculinity surely now he would move on to establish his virility.

Lionel was a fighter, not a lover, and when the hormones are raging and you've been putting out an invitation for free sex for three months with no takers, you tend to look for any port in a storm, and it was very stormy that night. So the film crew followed Lionel as he proceeded to drag his 'conquest' on his 'lek', intermittently making 'boom boom' with the carcass . . . for every one of the remaining six days of the shoot. Not surprisingly the crew wasn't looking to make a film about 'lekrophilia' so the entire ten days' footage remains unseen in a natural-history vault somewhere.

But what of Lionel? Well, if you go to the Kakapo Recovery Group website you'll find an entry for Lionel which reads: 'Lionel is thought to be infertile, so these days he lives on one of the Kakapo Team's back-up islands. Away from female company.' That's just the way Lionel likes it!

Thick as a brick

Just in case we embarrass anyone, let's just say this happened in a small South Island town, back in the days when appliances we now take for granted weren't all that common. A young fellow we'll call Greg, for argument's sake, was working in a hardware store, and had just been made responsible for the window displays.

He was very excited when the store took delivery of the town's first microwaves and video recorders, and proudly displayed one of each in the main window. That night someone threw a brick through the window and made off with the fancy new hardware.

The store owner called in the glazier, who suggested he look at reinforced glass, in case it happened again. 'Nah, mate,' he said. 'Lightning never strikes twice in the same place, I'll take my chances.'

Greg got another microwave and video from stock and redid his window display.

And the same thing happened. Someone put a brick through it in the middle of the night and they were minus another window and no sign of the second microwave or video.

This time the store owner took the glazier's advice,

and new reinforced glass was fitted. Something about locking stable doors after horses had already bolted was heard being muttered as Greg did his display for the third time.

About 3 a.m. the next morning Greg's phone rang. It was his boss, saying to meet him outside the store, as the police had called him and told him to get down there right away.

When Greg and the boss arrived, expecting the worst, the police were grinning from ear to ear. Out cold on the pavement in front of the shop was a man — with a brick lying beside him. The silly bugger had decided to have another go, only this time the reinforced glass bounced the brick back, hitting him between the eyes.

They got the missing gear back too, when he finally came round!

Bank inspector
Bill Jones

When a bank inspector called on a small country branch for a surprise audit he found the banking chamber deserted and the staff drinking beer in the manager's office. To teach them a lesson, he crept behind the counter and set off the hold-up alarm.

Much to his surprise, a barman from the pub next door immediately came running into the bank bearing a tray of fresh beers!

Not the Te Kuiti pages

Dianne Haworth

Towards the end of All Black Graham Purvis' celebrated playing career, which had taken him to most of the great rugby stadiums of the world, he turned out for Waikato in a pre-Super 10 fixture at the Taumarunui Domain in 1993. On finding there was no toilet paper in the players' lavatory, he sought out a King Country official. Could he help? The official dashed off to the committee room, returning a few minutes later.

There was no toilet paper there either, he apologised, as he handed Purvis the local telephone directory. 'Sorry, Purvey,' he said, 'this is the best we can do, but would you mind not using the Te Kuiti pages?'

Chainsaw

Martin Crump

We had just bought an overgrown half-acre with an old shed on it. This is down in the Coromandel, with a stream, and full-grown trees; idyllic you could say. For city dwellers this was our chance to get back in touch with the land. Get dirty, work hard, and sleep well from a hard day's work.

We were doing a bit of shopping in Whitianga and I was browsing around a second-hand shop where I found a pair of loppers for five dollars. Just what I needed to help clear the section. Excited with my purchase, we headed back to the good life and I started chopping everything in sight. The loppers were great, but not up to clearing a jungle, and they fell apart. Still, I wasn't disappointed as for a job this size I needed bigger equipment. I had a good sweat up; I jumped in the van, drove back to Whitianga and hired a chainsaw to make short work of it.

I'd used chainsaws before, so I didn't listen to the instructions I was given, and headed back. I got the chainsaw going, climbed the ladder and started cutting all the limbs off the trees. The light was coming back into our piece of paradise. I would have been going a good twenty minutes, when the chain wouldn't turn. The motor was going, but it wouldn't cut. There was sweat, sawdust, some foul language, anger and frustration as I drove the offending saw to the local garage who said they couldn't touch it as it was hired.

With my anger building, I make the drive all the way back to the hire place in Whitianga. I grabbed the chainsaw and walked menacingly to the counter, twigs and leaves in my hair, a very ugly face, smoke rising, a vein or two protruding from my neck and nobody else in the shop. The two guys serving were beginning to look uneasy. I banged the chainsaw down on the counter and said, 'It doesn't work and I've had to drive all the way back here!' I gave them THE LOOK and defied anyone to say the wrong word to me. All the guys in the shop had their backs to us or were ducking down behind the shelves. One of the staff leaned forward and pulled the brake back and said, 'It's fixed.'

The brake is a safety device while you're up ladders cutting down trees, and I'd knocked it on. The chuckles from around the shop were starting to grow as I picked up the chainsaw and turned. As I was leaving I said, 'Well, I'm good at other things.'

I got Jill to take the chainsaw back; I was still feeling stupid.

An unlikely genius

Dianne Haworth

Living on the West Coast in the 1940s there was a fellow who wandered the streets of Hokitika and was known to everyone by his first name of Donald.

Some accident in his early years or perhaps a hereditary defect had robbed him of a normal existence but he was a genius when it came to mathematics. Donald's fame grew and people would come from near and far to quiz him, asking seemingly impossible questions such as, 'Donald, what's 24 times 618?'

Donald would stare into the distance for a minute or more before solemnly replying 'Fourteen thousand, eight hundred and thirty-two.'

They would give him a ripper, some of the town's wags decided after a while, having worked out the answer in advance. 'Donald, how many times has the town clock struck the hour in the past eight years?'

Again the head to one side, again the answer.

'Wrong!' the townspeople replied triumphantly and repeated the story around Hokitika until they were brought to a halt by the town clerk.

'How many times did Donald say it was?' On being given Donald's answer the town clerk replied that he would check it out to make sure their 'genius' had for once got it wrong.

Some days later he came back with the reply. 'Donald was right. The town clock broke down four years ago and was out of order for several months until we got it repaired. Donald must have deducted that time off the total. His answer was 100% accurate.'

Smoker's cough
Don Morris

In 1938 I was a postman and one of my deliveries was to the farrier at the Auckland Trotting Club. On my way in to the entrance to the stables, I picked up a packet of yellow 'Three Castles' tobacco, which was one of the top brands. I didn't smoke this brand as it was too expensive.

When I got back to the Post Office after my deliveries, I told the postmaster of my find and he said he would buy it off me at a reduced price. The next day on my deliveries to the farrier, he asked me if I had enjoyed the smokes. I told him I had sold them to the postmaster. He laughed and said, 'Boy, you are in trouble — the packet we set up for you was a packet of horse manure.'

The postmaster wasn't amused and of course I had to repay the money and try to explain that the joke was supposed to be on me.

Weekend away
Martin Crump

Growing up, I didn't run into the old man all that often, but whenever I did there was usually an adventure in it somewhere.

I remember I would have been about eleven when he turned up out of the blue one time. He had a quick chat to Mum who then handed me an overnight bag and said, 'Have fun.' The next thing we're in the Land Rover heading south, to see an old mate of Barry's who lived in the bush on the other side of Rotorua. It felt like it was taking all day to get there — hot day, old Land Rover. We stopped once for a meat pie at a dairy somewhere. I remember being very thirsty, but I never said anything so I think I was reasonable company for my estranged old man.

We made it through Rotorua past the end of the sealed roads till two hours later we were on a dirt track deep in on a pot-holed, bush-covered dirt track. At the end of the track we grabbed our bags, got out and started walking. Barry seemed to know where he was going and he walked so fast I had to work hard to keep up. I could have wrung out one of my socks, I was so thirsty. We came across a path that led to our destination: a shack made of bits of iron and bush — on a lean, but built into a wonderful old oak tree. I liked it, just as I liked its occupier, Zac.

Zac was about sixty. He had no hair, but a full moustache and beard and from what I could make out, he had only about two teeth left, one on each side of his mouth. Zac asked us to sit down and did we want anything? I was so thirsty all I wanted was some water, but the old man grabbed a big jar off the shelf and started munching through its contents.

Barry and Zac did all the talking that evening while Barry kept munching his way through all the nuts in Zac's jar. When there was a break in the conversation I got to say a word.

'Zac,' I said, 'I hope you don't mind, but my dad has eaten his way through your whole jar of nuts there.'

'Not a problem, boy,' said the old fella. 'I love scorched almonds see, but me teeth won't let me chew 'em no more. A bloke was up here with a couple of packets last week, so I just sucked at 'em till I got the chocolate off and spat the rest in that jar there.'

You should have seen the look on Barry's face. I've never seen *that* story in any of his books!

Playing the joker

Brian Mackrell

My great-grandfather John Heslop was born in 1838 in the Cheviot Hills, a territory of wild borderers, the freebooters of Scots–English history. When he was eighteen he packed his few possessions on a swagstick and set off to see the world.

After some days' travel, he arrived at a wayside inn. The sun was setting as he staggered inside, dusty and exhausted, to ask for food and lodgings. The innkeeper told him that he had a hunting party of rich gentlemen staying so all the rooms were taken but one, which was haunted. Although the ghost had never made a physical manifestation, it had driven several lodgers screaming into the night with its demonic moaning.

John smiled and replied that he did not believe in ghosts, and that he would take the room. After a frugal meal, the weary youth climbed the stairs to the room and quickly fell into an exhausted sleep. He was soon rudely awakened by the return of the rowdy hunting party. The innkeeper told them of the country bumpkin who had paid for the ghost's room, which caused much hilarity among the party, who retired to a room beneath the haunted one to play cards. Made bold by the booze, they frequently bellowed to the youth upstairs to ask if he was enjoying himself with a ghost for company.

Their raucous performance only allowed John a fitful

sleep, but as midnight approached the gamblers became quieter — not for fear of ghosts but because most of them had passed out, slumped in a drunken stupor. A few hardened drinkers persevered with the cards and considerable amounts of gold passed across the table.

In the room above, young John began to sink into a deep sleep. Then, as he recalled years later, 'In the early hours of the morning, I heard a strange whispering. This gradually grew louder and more distinct. It's the ghost, I thought, and hardly dared to breathe.

'After what seemed an eternity, I plucked up the courage and jumped out of bed, and approached the nearest window to where the strange voice was coming from. I halted, I listened, I looked and still the voice moaned and whispered.

'Then I threw up the window, looked out, and the myth exploded. Outside the window was an old pear tree, trained against the wall. A branch was rubbing against the windowsill, being moved by a breeze which generally sprung up after midnight.'

Young John hastened back to bed. He was nearly asleep when a loud 'Hurrah!' from one of the hunting party disturbed him again. 'An idea entered my head. I wrapped a sheet around me and crept down the stairs. I approached the gambling den and slowly opened the door. At the sight of the moaning apparition in front of them, the gamblers let out yells and fled the room, leaving gold, cards and wine on the table.

'I had to laugh, but made the best of the opportunity, seized the gold and hurried back to bed. I was up at daybreak and met the trembling innkeeper on the stairs, who told me that for the first time the ghost had been seen. Needless to say, I lost no time in leaving the inn far behind me.'

A few more days on the road and John reached Liverpool, where the gamblers' gold was more than sufficient to buy passage to New Zealand.

The manner in which he claimed to have paid his way to the country, where he became known as 'Honest John', was not revealed until his 90th birthday, shortly before his death.

'You may say it was a doubtful proceeding on my part,' he told the audience at a function held in his honour, 'but the men were gambling. The pile of gold on the table went to the man who held the best hand. Some held kings, some held queens; but, well, I played the joker!'

Hard to swallow

Brian Noyes

I was having a drink with this home-brewer at the local pub when the publican called last drinks.

We'd put a few away but needed a roadie to clear the head. This was in the bad old days when bottle shops closed earlier than banks and it was looking pretty bleak.

Jim — well, that's what I'll call him in an attempt to keep his guilt anonymous — suggested I go back home and try one of his home-brews.

Now, other blokes had done this in the past and those who had survived the experience described a drink that, while alcoholic, was so bad not even the most hardened alcoholic could come near more than one. It had the odour of month-old witches' knickers and a flavour not unlike the slops that you find at the bottom of an abattoir's wheelie bin after a hot day.

I must've been a bit more pithed than I thought because somehow I found myself on the way back to Jim's house.

His horrible old wife greeted us at the door with a face that would scare Mike Tyson and an order that we take ourselves out to the back shed and not bother her or her equally ugly sister. Fat chance of that.

Anyway, Jim was also pleased to be banished to the shed and so we slunk through the house and made for the backyard.

Out in the shed he opened the fridge like a man opening a treasure chest. I swear the bottles were squirming and seething on the shelves and there appeared to be a foul green gas rising through the corroding tops.

Jim grabbed a bottle and then reached in the drawer for a bottle opener and a gun.

Yes, a gun.

Shit, I thought, he's gonna kill me.

'Don't be frightened,' said Jim. 'This is just to make sure we both have a nice drink.'

I was absolutely petrified as I didn't really know him that well and I was even more scared when he poured out a huge glass of this bubbling, burping, stenching, farting liquid and told me it was all mine.

'I, I, I, I might have lost me thirst, mate,' I said. 'I think I might've copped a poison pizza back at the pub.'

Jim went all strange and quiet. He looked at me, pulled the hammer back on the gun and pointed it at my temple.

'Drink the beer,' he said.

Trembling and gagging I raised the glass to my lips and apologised to God for being such a useless specimen, adding that I would never again get drunk, ignore the wife or ogle women if He let me out of this spot.

God is a bastard and I was forced to knock back the home-brew. Knowing not to sip, I threw it all down in one gulp.

I started to shake and sweat and everything spun for a while, but somehow I stayed on my feet and, despite feeling like a rat was decomposing in my stomach, I realised I was going to live.

Jim looked quite pleased about this and seemed to relax.

'Okay,' he said. 'Now it's your turn to hold the gun while I have a glass.'

Old Arch and his stroke
Daryl Crimp

The West Coast of the South Island is the birthplace of the rustic, archetypal and legendary characters, many of who reach larger-than-life status through the countless retelling of the classic Kiwi yarn. When living on the

Coast many years ago, I learned first-hand how such a character could achieve mythical status through a simple set of circumstances and the birth of another good yarn.

Much of the Coast in those days was governed by tradition and regularity; tradition being the need to drink at one of the many hotels and taverns, and regularity was measured by the number of days each week one frequented the said institution. Old Arch was so regular, never missing a session in a seven-day cycle, he was afforded his own stool in the corner of the bar and woe betide anyone silly enough to sit upon it.

Arch was a man of few words, content with his own company and muted conversation with a five-ounce draught. His head rested at an altitude of a little over five feet above sea level and his clothes hung limply from a bony skeleton that had never carried the bulk of an average man. He drank slowly and rhythmically, the bartender filling his jug without instruction whenever it emptied.

As is the case with all who imbibe, the call of the urinal has to be answered at some stage and it was still early when Arch shuffled through a smoke haze towards the gents. Conversation added to the atmospheric pollution and no one really noticed the old man's migration. Some twenty minutes later they did notice his absence from his stool in the corner, and inquisitiveness was overtaken by genuine concern when he didn't return to his half-completed beer.

Just as talk of a search party was gaining momentum the toilet door creaked open and Arch shuffled out, but not the Arch of half an hour earlier. This Arch was bent and dishevelled, twisted like a gnarled piece of driftwood — his right arm lifeless and deformed in front of his crotch. He shuffled with considerable difficulty and the bar fell quiet as he painfully dragged himself back onto his bar stool.

One of the patrons asked of him, 'Are you all right, Arch?'

'No, I'm bloody well not,' he sobbed, 'Can't ya see I've had a stroke?'

A pitiful murmur floated around the room and drinkers just stood and stared.

'I'm paralysed down my right side,' sobbed the old man. To a man, no one knew what to do, until a bloke standing closest to Arch made a startling observation.

'You silly old bastard,' he laughed, 'You've buttoned your cuff to your fly!'

Orange or green? The brawl's on!

Dianne Haworth

In the heyday of the 19th-century Thames gold rush, one annual happening drew the miners into town like no other. On each successive St Patrick's Day (17 March), Catholic-minded miners would walk or ride down from their mining camps to line up outside the Brian Boru hotel, while further down the main street the Protestant miners would similarly form their lines in front of Captain Butt's Hotel and American Bar.

One year it would be the turn of the Catholics, the next, the Protestants, to give the signal for an all-in battle via a barmaid seated on a horse and sporting a green (or orange if it was the Protestant's year) sash from shoulder to waist. The horse would be given a whack on the rump and the intrepid barmaid, green sash flying, would gallop down the street and into the enemy lines.

The public bar areas of both the Brian Boru and Butt's Hotel had been prepared for the big stoush, and makeshift bedding dotted their floors as the two pubs were transformed into hospitals to mend their wounded and injured supporters — Captain Butt's bar area was especially capacious, running to a huge 600 feet.

The St Patrick's Day fight became one of the spectacles of the year, drawing visitors by ship down from Auckland. Captain Butt, a man of the world, did handsomely out of the event by renting out his upstairs suites, where businessmen could discreetly entertain their ladies in style behind plush velvet curtains, providing a magnificent ringside and out-of-danger view of the carnage.

After a day of fighting and two days spent recovering, the miners were all best mates once more and returned happily together to their camps.

Ravishing Ruby

Martin Crump

I called my grandmother Ruby — not Nana, and certainly not Grandma, she hated that — so Ruby it was.

She stood no more than five foot one, full of spirit and life. We used to play slaps when we did the dishes together — that's where you try to slap each other on the face with an open hand, gently of course.

Ruby lived with us all my life until 1980, when she died at home aged seventy-eight. All those years she lived with us the family felt fortunate to have her love and support. She was feisty; she would let anyone know how she felt — good or bad — but she was very quick to laugh if there was no one around.

For thirty-four years Ruby worked in the office at the New Lynn Timber Company and leaning over a desk for so long had given her a hunched back. Despite this, Ruby was a great traveller and member of the Auckland Tramping Club and the Forest and Bird Society. This little lady from Sussex in England just loved the outdoors.

I was very lucky as a boy, for Ruby would take me tramping with her and together we walked the Heaphy, Routeburn, Milford and Hollyford tracks. I was aged between eight and eleven when we made these trips, but the memories are as clear as the photograph I still have of Ruby and me having a snow fight up the Tasman Glacier. I remember us sitting in our swimsuits next to a river in a small natural hot pool with large lumps of ice floating next to us.

I will never forget the Hermitage Hotel at the base of Mt Cook, although we're talking almost forty years ago now, so it can't have been open for long. We stayed at the Hermitage for three days. I remember I played in the lift and it was so luxurious I took a bath every day. The unusual thing is, like most nine-year-old boys, I hated baths. At home I used to sit on the edge of a full bath and splash my feet so that Mum would think I was in the bath having a good wash. Somehow it was different at the Hermitage.

There was a flash restaurant which Ruby thought would be a nice treat after we had been out walking one morning. We fronted up in our shorts, T-shirts and tramping shoes only to be sneered at by this gangly-looking thing, who looked us up and down and informed us that admission meant coat and tie for the gentleman and an evening dress for the lady. In the middle of the day! Ruby kicked up a hell of a fuss, telling the lemon-sucking creep in a suit that we were staying in the hotel and it was ridiculous that we were unable to come in and have a sandwich.

'No,' he said, 'I am the Maître D' and there are standards . . .' and on he went. Ruby wasn't backing down though and then a younger man, a waiter, came over and suggested we go outside onto the veranda. He settled us down at a table in front of the most magnificent scenery. The waiter brought Ruby and me a beautiful array of fresh sandwiches and cakes, plus a pot of tea, all on the house. Just what the doctor ordered. He had been charming and he had defused Ruby, which was no mean feat. In fact he should have been the Maître D'!

Well, that afternoon tea was the making of the trip. Ruby couldn't stop talking about it, especially the 'charming young man'. Although Ruby is not with us now, I haven't forgotten the walks, the sights, the game of slaps and the charming young man at the Hermitage.

Dick's pride and joy
Harvey Bell

In the late 1960s there were forestry camps scattered throughout New Zealand and Te Wera Forest Camp inland from Stratford in Taranaki was quite typical. Forest trainees (or technical trainees, as they were called) lived in these camps and were exposed to all sorts of unusual characters. Dick and Sam were trainees at Te Wera Forest Camp.

As the trainees were paid a very small salary, they didn't have much money after paying for the accommodation and cookhouse. One of the bugbears of living in isolated camps was the difficulty of getting to town to do the shopping. Sam had his motorcycle, but this wasn't much good in the rain with his best clothes on, and there was a fair chance of coming off in the loose metal, particularly after a jug of beer.

Dick, on the other hand, had saved fifty pounds

and decided to purchase some wheels. After much deliberation, he took the plunge and bought a Model A Ford pickup truck. This was his pride and joy as it gave him independence and was also useful as a shooting wagon along the forest roads.

Being permanently broke, Dick and Sam had trouble filling the Model A with petrol, which in those days was more expensive the further you lived from the big towns. Eventually Dick had an idea. 'Let's use a mixture of 50/50 petrol and diesel.' Diesel was half the price of petrol.

Down to the Te Wera General Store they went and filled her up with the 50/50 mixture. The store owner was quite amused and said it would never work and he called all of his customers outside to witness the blast off. Fortunately the Model A was still warm and the carburettor was full of petrol, so it took off as though nothing had changed, much to the disappointment of the gathered crowd.

However, about 200 yards down the road and around the bend, the old girl started to splutter and miss. Being the co-pilot, Sam thought quickly and pulled the choke halfway out and to their relief the motor ran quite well but with very limited power. Behind the old girl was a plume of black smoke pouring from the exhaust pipe. So far so good!

Next morning, Dick hopped in the cab and tried to start her, but no luck. As it was a work day, there was a Land Rover at the camp so a tow rope was produced and a mile-long tow commenced. Finally, the old girl spluttered into life and got them up to the office. Her permanent parking spots were on the steepest hills until such time as sufficient top-ups of petrol had diluted the diesel to the point where starting by battery could be achieved.

The Model A gave good service until one weekend when Sam wanted to borrow her to travel to Palmerston North to do some parachuting at the Manawatu Parachuting Club. He departed Friday night and on Sunday night had not returned.

On Monday at 8 a.m. Sam arrived at the office, having hitchhiked from the Toko Saddle. He didn't talk for the first hour at work even though Dick was questioning him as to the whereabouts of his pride and joy. When Sam finally told him what had happened, Dick was very distressed.

Sam had been negotiating the Toko Saddle at about midnight on a pitch-black night when the old girl's lights went out. Now anyone who had travelled the road would confirm that there was no hope of pulling up at speed on the metalled surface with no lights without hitting the bank or going over the edge.

Sam went over the edge, and by some miracle, the old girl came to rest on her side on the only patch of manuka for miles around.

Because it was totally dark and Sam didn't have a torch, he couldn't see where he was or what he was doing. He only knew that the Model A was perched very precariously, which was indicated by the fearful rocking which occurred whenever Sam moved. He decided to wait until help arrived or until daybreak about four hours later.

Because it was an isolated road, no vehicles passed by during the night. At daybreak, after a sleepless night, Sam gingerly climbed out of the old girl. This movement changed the centre of gravity and caused the old car to finally take off down the 300-foot hill into the gully below. She broke up into hundreds of pieces, some of which are probably still lying there today.

Dick got over the shock within a couple of days.

Sam has probably still not gotten over it.

Lost in translation

Rosina Panettiere

This is a story Billy T James had on one of his tapes about Dad. Billy T used to come into my Dad's fish shop in Cambridge as a young boy.

Dad had a fishing boat and was fishing away when the boat broke down. In those days years ago, they had the planes called Focker Friendships. Well, the plane circled over Dad's boat and kept saying, 'Focker Friendship, Focker Friendship, can you hear me?' They kept saying this for quite a while until Dad, being an Italian and not quite understanding them, yelled out with his hands waving in the air saying, 'I donna wanna your Focker Friendship, I needa your Focker help.'

I see the light

Martin Crump

I've tried my hand at many things but one of the more unusual set-ups was when I worked as an industrial spray painter. I took the job because it was close to home so I could walk to work.

There were twelve of us employed at the factory — eleven Pentecostals and myself. I'm sure I was only employed as a lost soul to be saved by my new colleagues. We ticked over all right for the first couple of months, but then I started to take a few liberties. Sleeping in a bit, missing the odd Monday and Friday, starting late and finishing early. I didn't feel too bad about this as they were always stopping themselves for prayer meetings that went through lunchtimes and beyond, then speaking in tongues or 'taking a burden', which left most of them running from the room in tears.

From what I understood, 'taking a burden' means putting everybody's sins and troubles onto yourself. I think some of their meetings were to try and save my soul. Once I watched three of them staring down a fly — trying to will it out of the room, for flies are evil apparently. I flicked my T-shirt at it and it stuck to the office window. I reckon my way was more effective.

One Friday morning at home as I was eating my breakfast I noticed in the paper that the Avondale

Races were starting that day at 1 p.m. I rang my mate and told him I would meet him there for the first race. I got to work a bit late, never mind, it was part of my master plan. If they wanted to help out and save souls then I would give them something to chew over.

At 11.30 a.m. I went to the manager's office with a dejected look on my face and told him of terrible goings-on at home between my mother and stepfather. Alcohol, violence, you name it. 'I'm beside myself,' I said, 'I can't concentrate on my work here. In fact, I should be at home.'

He gave me his blessing and off I went. He also told me to keep him informed of how things were going. By the way, my stepfather was a very kind loving man, so I took him along to the races with my mate. None of us did too flash though and the weekend wandered by. I had a nice little sleep-in on Monday morning, as I held an ace up my sleeve with these troubles at home.

So I get to work about 10 a.m. and everybody's got their heads down and won't look at me. You could cut the atmosphere with a knife, so I went to up one of them and asked what was going on. 'Bill the manager saw your car parked at the races when he went up to do the banking and he's not happy,' I was told. So I bowled straight into the manager's office with tears in my eyes and said, 'Gambling has got me, Bill, it's even got me lying to you!'

Well, he sat me down and told me about the evils of gambling and lying, right up until lunchtime. Perfect, only half a day to go. I told him the gambling had taken all my money, so he paid me for that morning too. What a lovely forgiving man. I think I'm beginning to see the light!

Lollywater
Ray Hardes

A friend of mine — we'll call him B2 to protect his identity — recently went on holiday and left the keys to his shed with a good friend. We borrowed a bottle of B2's home-brew, drank the beer and replaced the beer with cold tea and put the bottle back in his shed fridge.

After B2 had returned from holiday he was telling me that he had taken a few home-brews around to a friend's place at the weekend.

He said his friend keeps his beer glasses in the freezer and when he poured the beer it partly froze and tasted like lollywater.

'I don't know what went wrong, but I could not drink it,' said B2.

I managed to keep a straight face during all this and B2 did not suspect any foul play.

A week later, a group of us were playing cards and I took out a bottle of cold tea from the fridge. When I poured it into B2's glass, he tasted it and said, 'Hey, the same thing must have happened to your beer.'

From a great height

Maurice Flahive

On his first few days at the orphanage an eleven-year-old boy from the country met with many shocks and disappointments. He balked and choked on sticky, salty lumps in the breakfast porridge; the fatty lumps and broken rib bones floating in grease pretending to be Irish stew. He forced down the gritty, dark-brown sludge which the other boys called cocoa. 'You'll get used to it,' they told him.

Len, a boy of his age, with two years' residential experience in the Dunedin 1930s institution, was able to warn him about the harsh discipline of the place and give advice on avoiding the worst of it. 'Sorry, but you'll get a convict haircut just like mine.' The two formed a close friendship, which lasted a lifetime.

The orphanage manager was a tall, big-boned man with huge hands. It was soon evident that those hands meted out a frightening form of discipline.

On a hot, midsummer day, the boy was ordered to dig a large hole for the disposal of kitchen refuse and ashes. The job was arduous, toiling in the sun. As he took a rest, lying in the cool grass, he first heard and then saw something which reminded him of happier midsummer days at home: a skylark. His dreams soared high with the twittering lark and he fell asleep.

A kick in the ribs awoke him. As he jumped to his feet a heavy blow from the orphanage manager sent him sprawling into the hole he had dug. This time, as he came up he impulsively lifted the spade, either as a threat, or in defence, but the large hands reached out and took him by both ears, lifted him clear of the ground and shook him as a terrier would a cat.

That night the boy removed only his shoes before going to bed. When all was quiet he crept quietly from the building and ran barefoot through the city, taking the road to the mountains, the lake, home. A police car brought him back the next day.

The two nightshift constables who had picked him up from the highway, having observed the torn and bleeding earlobes, and the facial bruises, decided that the senior sergeant should know of this. Senior Sergeant Forbes, a brusque but kindly man, gently treated the boy's bruised face with hot towels and salve. 'What is the full name of this orphanage manager?' he asked.

'Jarred, sir,' the boy replied. 'I don't know his proper name but we call him Jockie.'

'Well now, boy', said the Senior Sergeant, 'you will go with the two constables and have a good breakfast. I'll drive you back to the orphanage. I have a few things to say to your orphanage manager.' Then to the constables, 'Somebody should come down hard on this Jarred joker, from a bloody great height.'

For some days the boy had to repeat his story. What the Senior Sergeant had said should be the fate of Jarred brought great delight. Young Geoff, lisping, became really excited. 'Pith on him. That's what the Sergeant means,' he exclaimed, actually jumping up and down at the thought of it. 'Pith on him, from a great height.'

There was, for a short time, a definite lull in the beatings and the boys now had a standard joke, which over and over again became a solace to the latest victim of Jarred's heavy hands. 'Pith on him,' they would say. 'Pith on him from a great height,' and all would fall about laughing, including the latest victim.

At the age of eighteen the boy had become a man. At least he was doing a man's job, serving 'up north' in the wartime Air Force. On his first leave pass he travelled south, stopping off at the city where he looked up his old friend Len, also doing a man's job as a wharfie. 'I hope you haven't stopped off to make a friendly visit to old Jockie,' Len chided. 'The old bugger dropped dead ten days ago. He's under the sod where he belongs.'

They spent the afternoon at the St Kilda pub reminiscing, laughing and drinking eight-ounce beers. At six o'clock closing time, the two young men left the pub, each with two bottles of beer in a brown paper bag, and staggered up the road to Andersons Bay cemetery.

Next morning they stood together in the Magistrate's Court, charged with disorderly behaviour. 'We responded at 6.45 p.m. last evening to reports of two men behaving strangely at the Andersons Bay cemetery,' stated the prosecuting sergeant.

'What disorderly things were they doing at the cemetery?' asked the Magistrate.

'The two men were found at the grave of one John L Jarred, recently deceased. They had placed empty beer bottles and dandelions on the grave.'

'Is that all, sergeant?'

'No, your Honour. They had entered the implement shed from where they removed two forty-gallon drums. When the responding constables arrived the two defendants were standing high on the upturned drums urinating on the grave of Mr Jarred.'

The Magistrate took a very stern look at the two young men over the top of his spectacles. 'It seems to me, sergeant, that a more serious charge should be entered here.'

'It was considered,' replied the sergeant, 'but Inspector Forbes knows of the relationship of the defendants to the deceased Mr Jarred. May I approach the Bench, Your Honour? I have a note from the Inspector explaining what, in his opinion, are mitigating circumstances in this case.'

A thief's hobby

Bernard Skitt

The landlord of my local pub was standing behind his lounge bar polishing glasses as he watched a lady customer surreptitiously sliding beer mats from the table into her handbag.

'Would madam care to come to the bar? I will happily supply her with a complete selection of my beer mats rather than she clears them from the tables,' he called across the crowded bar.

The rather embarrassed lady made her way to the bar and stood before him, thanking him for being so kind.

'There must be a name for a collector of beer mats such as myself,' she said.

'There is, madam,' he replied in a stern voice. 'A common bloody thief.'

One out of the box
Briar Marshall

This is about my dad, Reg Phillips, a character who loved life, especially the outdoors: fishing, hunting, dog trials, including farming and bird rearing.

Dad always had a knack of getting out of jobs he disliked. Mum once thought she could get him to do the dishes. He dried the cups and saucers and then put them in the flour Mum kept in big bins. The knives and forks went in the bins of sugar and the plates went under the bed. He was never asked to do the dishes again.

Mum sometimes went to the pictures or the odd meeting with neighbours (having a dairy farm, Dad never went out much in the evenings). On arrival home, Mum would open the door to jam spread on the light switches, so she didn't turn them on, and cotton (from cotton reels) hooked across the room, from door knob to door knob, picture to picture. Anything and everything was draped in cotton. Mum was left with jam and cotton caught up in such a mess she didn't know where she was! She didn't go out in the evenings much from then on.

Fortunately, Mum had a wonderful sense of humour and they complemented each other well with lots of laughter and fun.

Dad bred Labradors, mainly black dogs, and was involved in the local gun dog club. He was President and Mum was Secretary, and they also had an interest in rearing pigeons, pheasants, chooks and all manner of caged birds. The local boys used to come and ask to buy pigeons off Dad. He would tell them to keep the pigeons caged for two to three weeks, to keep them from homing back to him.

However, most times the pigeons would fly back home to Dad! A day later the boys would turn up saying, 'Mr Phillips, we lost those birds. Have you got any more?'

'Yes, of course, of course, there's plenty,' Dad would say and sell them back the same birds! He always kept in touch with them to ask about feeding and watering and gave them back their money — but not before getting a good laugh out of it.

On your mower

We had just purchased a small lifestyle block of five acres and one of the first items we required was a ride-on mower. Not knowing much about these, I had a good look at many brands and models before deciding which one was best for us and within our price range.

The first on the list was a John Deere — very nice, but possibly a bit more mower than we needed. Next, I considered a Ranger, well built, but the model for us was not available for another two weeks. Then, I discovered that one of our old friends, Lance, was selling ride-on mowers, so around I went. He gave me a deal that had me writing out the cheque there and then, before he changed his mind. This brand, a Viking, looked every bit as good as the others.

Lance delivered the new flash Viking mower the next day. My wife had been to town after she had been told the name of the mower and bought a two-horn hat just like the Vikings wore from the $2 Shop, for me to wear while on the mower. She said that if I had bought a John Deere mower, she would have had me wear the reindeer antler hat from our last Christmas party and if I had brought the Ranger mower home, she would have had me wear my Stetson.

'Good thing I didn't purchase a mower from my mate Reg,' I said.

'Why's that?' she asked.

'Because he sells another well-known brand called Cox.'

Beer and marriage
Winston Lau

Back in 1995, I was living by myself and one day I happened to see a cooking programme on television. They were making 'Fish and chips with a twist'. The 'twist' was adding a can of your favourite chilled beer to the batter. They also showed you how to make the side salad.

After watching the programme and taking note of the recipe, I went to buy the ingredients at my local supermarket. I collected all the necessary ingredients and placed them on the checkout counter. I then noticed that the person in front of me had the same kind of ingredients: flour, eggs, vegetable oil, tomatoes, baby spinach, Spanish onions and a deli parcel wrapped in white paper. Surely it wasn't fish?

It was uncanny, bizarre, and it couldn't possibly have been the same recipe. That's what I was telling myself anyway, hoping that no one else would notice.

How embarrassing.

I had a quick glance at the lady in front of me and just smiled. I don't think she knew what was happening. I finally paid for my groceries and left the supermarket in a hurry.

I was still missing one ingredient — the beer — so I entered the local bottle shop, grabbed a can from the fridge and went to the counter.

Lo and behold, I saw the same lady with the same beer as was used on the television programme. It was also the same as the one I had in my hand.

My suspicions were confirmed.

She was quite attractive and me being a bloke, I couldn't let the opportunity pass by. I started a conversation with her and found out that she also saw the TV programme and yep, she was cooking for her parents that night.

Somehow I managed to ask her out and eight months

later we got married. Every year since, we have celebrated our anniversary with 'Fish and chips with a twist'.

The caravan
Sally Downing

A retired couple had owned a caravan for some years, a fact that grated on the lady as the 'van' wasn't used much. After much nagging they set off for places south. A couple of nights passed in the National Park and tempers hadn't improved. In desperation the husband decided home was better and set off with his wife asleep in the caravan.

Reaching the Desert Road about 6.30 a.m. he pulled over to relieve himself. Unbeknown to him, his wife felt the same urge. He finished his communication with nature and drove off. His wife, clad in nightie and housecoat, was left freezing on the side of the road.

The first vehicle to come past was a motorbike. The young man agreed to try and catch up with the caravan, taking the lady pillion. Some thirty minutes later they overtook the van. Husband sees wife, nightie in full flight, helmet over rollers, and drives off the road, rolling the caravan and nearly their car. The wife was restored to her husband.

They gratefully thank the biker and call AA rescue. The result: caravan — write-off; car — a little damaged; couple — thank their lucky stars and opt for motels.

Counting sheep
Chris Horneman

There's a story in our family about Dad not being able to sleep. He would lie there at night, tossing and turning. Mum suggested counting sheep, but that didn't work. In frustration she said, 'If you can't sleep and you can't count sheep, try counting glasses of beer; that should come naturally to you.'

A few seconds passed and Dad got out of bed.

'Where are you going?' asked Mum.

'To get my first beer,' said Dad.

But wait, it gets worse
Denise Roche

My brother told me a story recently. A true tale of pettiness, unreasonable clients, upset families and it involved a digger, rain and a cemetery. The story got worse and worse and as it escalated and as I repeatedly exclaimed, 'Oh, no!', he said, quite calmly: 'But wait, it gets worse.'

This is my But Wait, It Gets Worse story.

My dearest man travels a lot, and survival skills are a requirement for where I live on the farm out the back of Waiheke Island. Our life is what you'd definitely call 'alternative' and it's taken a lot of learning to get used to it. It's not just the solar and wind twelve-volt electrical system (that I found out could be totally blown up if you attempt to do the ironing) or the tank-water system (pumps can break down leaving no access to running water) or the feral free-range chicken population (and there was that time I had to finish off killing the rooster after the dog ran amok with them) and let's not even mention the long drop. When faced with some of these problems while John's been away I've occasionally shed a couple of tears in self-pity but have always been resourceful. Actually, on reflection, I've been the epitome of stoicism.

But this time I cracked.

John went to Canada on Thursday leaving me and our daughter and Zac the aged dog back on the farm. Zac is a reformed chicken killer and has subsequently had a productive life dealing to the rodent and rabbit population on the farm. He's now fifteen and grey in the muzzle and looks like he may have taken voluntary retirement.

At this time of year on the farm it is definitely rodent season. The weather is getting cooler and all those little field mice and bush rats are looking for somewhere warm to live and it's not really that uncommon on Waiheke for locals to have to deal with the occasional rat or mouse. We put poison out and a couple of traps and usually Zac helps. In this way we'd dealt to quite a few of the creatures and I've become quite proficient at smelling out dead rats and disposing of their bodies. I usually just fling them over into the paddock and let the hawks have a go at them.

After John left I'd flung three rats over the fence in the space of two days. One had got into the laundry cupboard so I'd also spent a wet weekend washing all the sheets and towels.

On Sunday night my daughter and I came home from a girls' afternoon out that had run on to dinner, to find a rat in the kitchen drinking the leftovers from the bottom of my coffee cup. Instead of squealing (that would be bad role-modelling) I grabbed the egg slice and opened the window and tried to shoo it out. The rat looked up from the cup and then avidly slurped some more coffee before launching itself onto the top shelf where it was both out of reach and hidden. I grabbed the broom handle and started poking until it ran around the ceiling and launched itself behind the fridge. Despite my shrieking 'Kill it! Kill it!', Zac stayed on his bean bag and ignored the excitement. Given that the rat and I had reached an impasse, I decided to hope the rat would leave the house and went and put my daughter to bed.

But the rat didn't leave. While reading the bedtime story we heard the crashing of broken glass. Then more slurping. In his eagerness to get back to the coffee cup, the rat had run across the shelves holding the wine glasses, tipping one of them off the shelf in its travels.

When my child was safely asleep I went back into the kitchen and swept up the glass. I couldn't see the rat, although there was still some coffee in the cup. I thought maybe it had left. I listened closely for a while and thought I could hear it outside. 'Phew,' I thought, 'crisis over,' and promptly popped myself into bed. I could hear rat-rustling but was pretty convinced that it was outside my window.

I was wrong. The rat was actually inside, as I found out when it jumped onto the foot of my bed. I got a hell of a fright — and so did the rat as we both kind of squeaked at the same time. It scurried under the bed at the same time as I was flinging myself out of bed and grabbing the first weapon to hand. Unfortunately the said weapon was only a water bottle and the rat avoided the missile easily.

'Rat! Rat!' I shouted at Zac, who wearily heaved himself out of his bean bag just in time to ignore the rat crossing the floor to skulk under the sofa. I grabbed a torch so was able to see its little beady eyes shining in the beam, which clearly disturbed the rat somewhat as it came shrieking out from under the sofa and launched itself to the top of the bookshelf.

By this time my heart was palpitating and my hands were trembling and by the sounds of it the rat was in pretty much the same state as he careered across the ceiling beams in an effort to escape my torch light. He eventually made it back into the kitchen and the top shelf again as another wine glass crashed to the floor.

'Bugger it,' I thought. 'I'm certainly not going to clean up glass while there's a manic hyped-up-on-caffeine rat in there.'

I'd had enough. Taking solace in the fact that I am a human — with a big brain — I finally formulated a plan. I retrieved the rat trap from the garage and cunningly positioned it between the coffee cup and the fruit bowl just underneath the shelf with the glasses. Then I turned out the lights and gingerly got back into bed, checking under the bed first with the torch.

After a nerve-wracking half an hour I heard another glass shatter in the kitchen. 'Damn,' I thought. 'We've only got one left.' About five minutes later the trap snapped.

'Got ya!' I thought smugly to myself and settled down to wait a few minutes so that I would have to deal with a dead rat, as opposed to a dying one. My victory was short-lived, however, since the next sound was the banging of the trap and an angry squealing from the rat. It didn't stop.

Eventually I realised that the rat was not going to die any time soon and so I was forced to investigate. Sure enough, there was the rat, dragging the trap by his foot, trying to dislodge it by squeezing himself between the oven and the bench.

'Damn!' I said, or words to that effect, not only because I was still having to deal with the rat but also because I'd neglected to put shoes on and the floor was awash with shards of glass.

In a frenzy I raced off and found the flounder spear and raced back into the kitchen to dispose of the damn rodent.

Reality is somewhat different to novels, however — as I found out as I stabbed and missed and stabbed and missed the frantic and squealing rat. Eventually I put some newspaper down on the floor and with my foot (now shod I might add) pushed the rat onto the paper and held it in one place by standing on the end of the trap. Taking a big breath I plunged the spear down. And bloody missed again. Swearing and feeling a bit sick I decided to forgo the big plunge and just positioned the tip of the spear — which was not really that sharp — on the rat and pushed down with all my weight. Rat stopped moving.

'Great,' I thought and removed the spear, only to find the rat alive and more frantic than ever and drops of blood scattering on the newspaper. 'Oh, bloody hell,' I said and had another go at spearing the rat. The rat stayed still on the end of the spear but I realised it was still breathing even though it looked like it was mortally wounded.

Feeling somewhat frantic myself I grabbed the nearest knife to hand and tried to will myself to put the little bugger out of its misery. The knife was a serrated bread-knife and as I pointed it closer and closer to the rat's neck I suddenly realised that I was going to have to saw its head off. That's when it finally, irrevocably, occurred to me that I am a complete and utter wuss. I promptly threw up all over the floor.

I couldn't do it, I just couldn't. I grabbed the spear, the trap and the rat slung between them and sprinted over to the paddock where I released the rat from both torture devices with a whispered apology for its pending slow painful death.

My apology was heartfelt. I did feel sorry for the rat. I had time to reflect on its rather sweet little face and unpleasant death as I spent the next hour or so cleaning up the broken glass, blood and vomit off the floor. It's just its behaviour I didn't like. I guess you could blame that on the coffee.

I got to bed eventually at about one o'clock, exhausted and wrung out, and I spent all night starting awake at every noise. In the morning I bought $70 worth of rat traps and poison and put them on John's account at the hardware store.

When John phoned later to see how things were I encouraged him to go shopping. I think I deserved something really, really expensive and exquisite.

Boy-scout training

Percy Allison

Tim was a cook-cum-shepherd down in the South Island's Mackenzie country. Being miles from camp, the usual practice was to take along a billy to boil water, adding sugar and tea. This particular day, they arrived in the tussock country to find not a tree or twig in sight, just clumps of tussock grass every two or three feet apart.

'Well, this is a nice how do you do!' said Tim's mate. 'Not a blinkin' piece of stock to boil the billy.'

'Hold on a minute,' said Tim, 'I wasn't a boy scout for nothing. If a bloke can boil a billy using snow water on the Klondyke or dried camel dung in the desert to cook for a whole camel train — this is a piece of pie to me. Now all you gotta do is light a clump of tussock and while I hold the billy over it for the ten-second burst of flame, you light the next clump in line and I'll follow you as quick as I can.'

Away they went, going great guns, burning up the countryside as they went.

But by the time the billy boiled, they were five miles from camp and both had forgotten the tea!

Exciting moments in a Chevrolet

Doug Curtis

When I joined the staff of Ormond's Motors Limited, Gisborne, as an apprentice motor mechanic, I was very privileged to have the use of our family car. This particular Chevrolet had no brakes fitted to the front axle and with the external rear brake bands open to the elements, there were times in wet conditions when it virtually had zero brakes. An open tourer with a canvas hood, it was a very basic model.

In 1948, I used to travel most weekends to Waimana in the Bay of Plenty to visit my brother Jack and his wife Ella, where they lived on a station Jack managed for the Lands and Survey. This meant a considerably long trip through the Waioeka Gorge to Opotiki and then on to Waimana. The gorge road was a long single-lane road of clay and rock, with odd patches of river shingle, a raging river far below on one side, and a high cliff face on the other side.

This particular time my sister Colleen came with me. All went well and after a slow trip over Trafford's Hill we entered the gorge and were coping well with the twisting road. About this time I noticed a Citroën car, towing a trailer, coming up fast behind us and making a lot of dust. I said to Colleen, 'Hang on, I am going to speed up and try and keep ahead of the dust.'

I started to chase a bit more out of the old Chev. The old car responded well and we really got cracking until a corner came up and I suddenly realised the old bugger was bolting. Even with my foot right off the throttle we were still gaining speed. I hurriedly moved all the hand controls that these early vehicles had, with no response. Finally I turned off the ignition and steered to a passing spot. The engine stopped and the Citroën and trailer went past without so much as a friendly wave. The driver probably thought I was playing silly buggers.

After a couple of minutes of silence, I said to Colleen, 'She bolted on me.' Colleen was very white and shaking. I climbed out and lifted the bonnet to check what had happened. All appeared to be in order so I asked Colleen to put her feet on the floorboards. She did and the throttle went to the full open position. Unbeknown to either of us Colleen had been operating the throttle from her side of the car. The more nervous she became the more pressure she put on the floorboards and the faster we went.

I made poor old Colleen travel all the rest of the way to Waimana with her feet on the seat. I spent quite a large part of my weekend making new floorboards so that we could return to Gisborne. Some of you may recall the Waioeka Gorge in the 1940s before it was widened and sealed. It was certainly no road or place to be driving a vintage Chevrolet at forty to fifty miles per hour.

The match

Patricia O'Leary

Our William told a story of a time in the sticks, when children ran barefoot and people were 'bricks'.

When Winston McCarthy was an announcer of note, he refereed boxing and punted the tote.

In a hick country town, not far from here, behind the bar Winston was serving a beer.

Two warring factions lived near the town. When they saw each other, the locals would frown.

They'd rush from the place, or hide in the bar, but wherever they went, it was sure to be far.

The air was hushed, the air was silent. The Layhies and Brumninskys were looking quite violent.

'There'll be trouble tonight!' was on every lips, the township agog, the betting on tips.

The bar door burst open, all eyes were still. The electrified air exploded in 'kill'.

Two policemen there sauntered out to the door, they looked down the street and then looked some more.

With arms quietly folded, they heard not a sound

— not even when a body bounced on the ground.

Our quick-witted Winston had jumped on a table and refereed the match as he was brilliantly able.

The first round to the Brumninskys, the second was fouled, the third was a draw with a penalty eye gouged.

A left to the chin, a smash to the eye, a deep undercut and a punch way too high.

A head butt was out, and so was a bite as they fisted and wrestled well into the night.

The bar tap flowed freely with light amber ale and at each point scored the crowd cheered, without fail.

At the last round, he came to the pair. 'Shake hands,' he said, 'the winning was fair.'

In a brotherly hug, they admitted defeat and the two warring factions went back to their sheep.

The reluctant house cow

Maurice Flahive

A really nice old guy called Mick told me of a time when, as a young married man, he came to work at Kawhia for the local council in the early 1930s. He had come from the city where they delivered milk to a billy at the door. He didn't like having to walk a couple of miles across paddocks for his daily milk, so he let it be known at the council meeting that he had a side paddock and a long-acre at the gate, ideal for a house cow. A big brown-and-white cow, in full milk, was duly delivered to him.

Mick came home from work that day, grabbed a bucket and stool from the house and headed out to the paddock to collect from his new milk supply. The cow had different ideas.

Mae, as she was subsequently named (after another large lady of the same era), was born and raised on 400 acres, part of a herd of fifty. To show this stranger her displeasure at being penned in half an acre with not another cow in sight, she lowered her head, bellowed with rage and charged. Mick was quickly through the fence but he left the shiny bucket behind, so, two bunts and a toss to that before she buck-jumped to the far end of the paddock to stand snorting and blowing steam clouds from her nostrils.

Each of several more attempts that evening and the next day had Mae bucking like an unbroken brumby or charging like a Spanish bull.

'You'll have to send her back,' said Mick's missus.

'You'll have to get a calf to drink all that milk,' said the kids from next door.

'Nothing I can do for her,' said the vet.

'I'll give you seven quid for her,' said the butcher.

'Why doncha tie her up, legs and all,' said Dopey Donald.

'Who's going to catch her, Donald?' asked Mick, condescendingly.

Everybody condescended to Donald.

'The policeman will lasso her,' cried Donald,

jumping up and down with glee at the thought of it.

The local policeman of the time was a real character, a giant of a man. No patrol car, not even a bicycle for him. His official mode of transport was a horse. He sat tall in the saddle like a Texas Ranger and carried a lariat at the saddle horn. There was very little crime for a big strapping cop to deal with so he welcomed a chance to show off.

What a performance it was, better than a latter-day rodeo. All the local kids turned up, and half the adults. The constable rode up dressed in full uniform, dismounted and placed his helmet on the fence post, then, disregarding the cow, proceeded to educate and entertain the gathering. First he demonstrated how to tear some long fabric strips from an old garment and plait the parts to make a halter, just the right shape and size for a cow's head. This was followed by a display of lariat twirling and lasso throwing that would have put Buffalo Bill to shame. An hour after his arrival he donned his helmet, remounted, directed Mick to open the gate and, amid cheers from the kids, rode in to confront the recalcitrant cow.

Mae was cropping grass in the centre of the paddock and jumped backwards, greatly surprised at the gigantic apparition approaching. She retreated to the back fence. The apparition kept coming. The lariat whirled around the helmet, then, whoosh, the rope snaked out and the noose dropped over her shoulders. The horse leaned back; the rope tightened. Mae tried to run down the fence-line, the rope pulled her sharply around. This was too much. She lowered her head and charged right between the front legs of the horse. Cow, horse and constable went down in a sprawling heap, kicking, mooing, whinnying, cursing. Mick, the vet and the butcher rushed in, grabbed the rope, took a few turns around the cow's legs, then sat on her while the limping, still cursing policeman put his plaited halter in place.

There followed the most undignified milking. Tied as she was, head and front legs to the gatepost, while two men held the back-leg ropes, Mae still managed to knock Mick off the stool twice and the bucket over once. She was released at dusk with the plaited halter still in place. The population went home and fully agreed that today's was the best show the town had turned on for years.

It rained cats and dogs that night and was still raining when Mick ventured gingerly into the paddock next morning. To his surprise, and the disappointment of the kids gathered to watch, the cow stood like a statue, head bowed as if in shame, and completely ignored the whole milking performance.

Mick was surprised at the morning's events but amazed when he found the cow still standing in the same place that evening, and all of the next day. Mae had not eaten a blade of grass, the milk had about run out, and although she was dragged to the water tub she would not drink. Saturday morning came and the whole populace (well almost) gathered again at Mick's gate.

'She's sulking 'cos I got her beat,' said the policeman.

'She'll have to go back to the herd,' said Mick's missus.

'She looks like she's going to die,' said the kid from next door.

'Nothing I can do for a cow on a hunger strike,' said the vet.

'I'll give you three quid for her,' said the butcher.

Dopey Donald had made a close inspection of the cow's front end about this time then waited patiently to get a word in.

'It's no wonder she won't eat or drink,' he said when his chance came. 'The rain has shrunk the policeman's halter so it's too bloomin' tight around her jaws. She couldn't even say moo if she wanted to!'

Well, you did ask . . .

A farmer was swamp ploughing in the wopwops near Monowai when he hit a larger than usual stump. The plough was rendered useless.

The man applied for insurance so he could replace it. When the claim form came, among other questions was 'name witnesses'. After the farmer thought for a while, he wrote down 'two rabbits and a swamp hen'.

He had the plough replaced!

Tikitiki on the East Coast

Doug Curtis

When I worked on the East Coast doing vehicle inspections for the Transport Department, I used to stay at the Tikitiki Hotel. We did our vehicle inspections in Syd Yates' garage, right next to the hotel, which was very convenient. After we finished for the day, we made a beeline for a beer that was on between five o'clock and six in those days. The evening meal was at 7 p.m. and afterwards we met up with the others staying in the hotel, in the private bar of the hotel.

I met a wool, skin and dag buyer, who was also staying over, and an Irishman named Tom Dargie. It just happened to be Tom's 60th birthday so after quite a few of Tom's whisky shouts and a late-night supper in the publican's kitchen, I retired to my bedroom and lay on my bed.

I didn't lie down for long as the room appeared to be moving and I felt the need to put my head near a toilet bowl. Back I went to my room feeling like death. I lay down fully dressed and must have dozed off. When I awoke I decided I'd better have a bath and try and get right for the day ahead. I entered the huge bathroom and flopped into it with both taps running.

God knows how long I slept but I woke to find both taps still running and I was shivering like a dog. I stepped out of the bath and spread myself across the lead floor. I had forgotten it was an old-fashioned bath mounted on high legs. I turned off the taps and pulled the plug as the water was flowing over the edges and across the floor, and had been for some time. I was still shivering as I dried myself off with a huge white hotel towel and then decided to use this towel to mop up the water on the floor. When I hung it back up I noticed it now was black from the lead on the floor.

Next morning, feeling like death, I decided I had better have some breakfast and try and recover my strength. I entered the dining room and sat sheepishly at a table. A very large and smiling Maori girl in a beautiful white starched dress said to me so all in the dining room could hear, 'Did you have some trouble in the bathroom last night, Pakeha?' I nodded and she continued, 'Yes, we have no hot water. You drained the cylinder.'

Had I been staying in the hotel the night it burnt down recently, I might have saved it with all the water that flowed out of the bath that night!

'Is that you, Battler?'

Nina C

I was brought up in Kohuratahi, a small farming community about 10 km east of the famous Whanga-momona. In the 1930s and 40s, long before power reticulation, we communicated amongst ourselves and with the outside world via the telephone.

Several settlers shared a party line which was given a number. For example, ours was the No. 8 line and our calling code was K. So a long–short–long ring on the phone was ours. This morse-code dialling system was operated manually by using the crank handle on the phone and this in turn charged the batteries that powered the bells. If we wanted to call a family on a different line we had to phone the local central exchange, who would then connect us, if that line was free! There'd be any number of subscribers on any one line, so it was a case of pot luck when sending and receiving calls. To enable others on the line to know when you'd finished a conversation, etiquette required you give an abrupt little ring. If you picked up the receiver to make a call and found it 'working', you would say sorry and hang up and wait for them to finish. If there was an emergency you butted in to their conversation and they'd let you have the line.

In such a small, close-knit community, where just about everyone was related or connected to everyone else, gossip and news were paramount.

By very gently lifting the phone receiver so that it didn't make a click, and by keeping background noise to a deathly quiet, you could listen in to others' conversations without being detected. This was a particularly popular method of finding out what prices neighbours got for their wool and stock sales when the stock firms phoned in from Stratford.

Local gossip, illness, crisis and who was doing what with whom were also popular topics.

Now we had in our district an elderly fellow called Battler. He lived a lonely bachelor life down a remote valley and was hungry for neighbourly contact. He was terrible at listening in to private conversations and annoyed others on his line no end. Two lady friends decided they'd had enough of Battler's eavesdropping and couldn't resist the temptation to catch the old fellow out. So in the middle of their next conversation to each other, one said suddenly, 'Is that you, Battler?' Without thinking and caught totally off guard, he replied, 'Yes', and his game was up — well, for that day anyway!

Caught in the act
Jack Stafford

A drover always worked things out to stop at a small place where a pub was situated only about half a mile from the holding paddocks on his drive. He settled the stock and wandered down for an evening's drinking.

There was a barmaid that he found most salubrious and he chatted her up. She was accommodating and told him to leave the pub then sneak back. She gave him the number of her room and warned him to be very careful as the publican also fancied her.

He made a few comments about being tired and noisily left the bar. After walking up the road for a way he sneaked back, found her room, stripped off and got into bed.

After the bar closed the little beauty joined him for savage satisfaction and this was followed by deep sleep for them both. They awoke to the sound of pots and pans clattering, and noise from voices including much laughter. She kicked him out at high speed and with an armful of clothes he gently opened the door. Lying there patiently waiting for him was the cause of the laughter. Four of his faithful dogs had come looking for him during the night when he never came back to the stock and had no trouble locating him. Once they had settled down to wait, nobody else had any trouble knowing where he was either.

Rainbow trout for tea

Maurice Flahive

My red-headed mate, Bob, and I, as ten-year-old hunter-gatherers, took two 'good-feed' sized rainbows from the Gorge Road creek by a much practised method of trout tickling. We hung the two fish by the gills on a long stick and marched home through the town, with our catch shoulder high calling and waving to townsfolk we knew. Mr Alf Atley, the Council water engineer, waved back and called to us, but we just waved again and marched boastfully on home.

It was near teatime; I was already seated at the table, knife and fork at the ready. My large trout was frying in the pan when my mother went to answer a loud knock on the door.

'Oh, hello, Constable Roycroft, come on in.' My mother never left anyone standing at the door.

'No, thanks all the same, Isobel,' said the constable, breathing deeply through his nose to sample an inviting aroma of trout frying in butter.

The rest of the conversation had me on full alert ready to hide under the table, or maybe escape out the front door. The constable explained that Alf Atley was an honorary ranger of the Acclimatisation Society and responsible for licensing and control of trout fishing. He has reported seeing two local lads, this day, with two large trout carried on a stick, obviously poached from the creek.

'There was one lad with ginger hair, he was certain of by name, but the other, he just thought that maybe, he was your middle boy. But I can't act on maybe, can I? Just let him know anyway, Isobel, that it is unlawful to take trout from the creek without a licence and small boys don't qualify for a licence. Enjoy your tea.'

The message to my good mate Bob and his mother was made much simpler. The policeman met Bob's young sister as he approached their house.

'Hello, young lady. How are you today?'

'I'm fine thank you, Mr Roycroft. We're having trout for our tea,' Bob's sister Betty said gleefully. 'Our Bobby caught it in the Gorge Road creek.'

Our dog Flash and the postman

Ngaire Ellwood

There were ten of us kids and growing up together in Foxton was fun. Our biggest treasure back when we were kids was our good old mate Flash, the family dog.

Flash was an Irish water spaniel. He went every-where us kids went and was just like one of us. While we were in school Flash would wander off from the school gate and spend time fossicking in the bins around town as he made his way home to Union Street to sleep in the sun. After school everyone in town knew that if they saw Flash, there would also be some of us kids around, at least three or four of us.

Boydie the postman never truly understood Flash. Although we sometimes had other posties from time to time in Foxton, Flash seemed to know when Boydie was on the mail round and he would lie in wait. Flash never took any interest in any other postman — only Boydie.

Everywhere else in town Boydie would blow his

whistle when he put mail into mailboxes, but he never blew his whistle near our place. Boydie knew that Flash was waiting for him so he used to come around the corner from Johnston Street into our street and immediately start winding up.

Boydie would pedal madly and go speeding past our house on his bike at what seemed to us kids to be about fifty miles per hour, and throw the mail into the mailbox, hardly changing his pace.

Flash would hide around the corner of our house, seemingly very relaxed, but would be up at a run, out the gate and up the road after Boydie at a great pace the moment the mail was safely in the box. He never caught Boydie, just chased him for 100 yards and then sauntered home.

I swear Flash used to go down to the post office from time to time to check the roster to see when Boydie was on. He would lie around the yard for days not even twitching when any other postman was working, but once Boydie was on the mail round, away Flash would go again.

Boydie has passed away now, but he was a very fit man and I still maintain to this day that he has Flash to thank for all the cardiovascular exercise he regularly got.

A new way of milking

Pat Conaglen

The following events took place on a South Taranaki farm sometime in the 1950s.

Poor young Laurie wanted to be an electrician and had little desire to be a farmer. However, his widowed mother insisted that he come home and run the family dairy farm, which he dutifully did.

The farm, as it turned out, was soon ablaze with bright lights and had motorised gates and Laurie had even invented the cattle prodder before it was invented.

One day his cousin, Ryan, who lived across the road, heard one hell of a commotion coming from Laurie's cowshed and thought he had better go and investigate. Looking over the rails he saw Laurie with a cow upside down in a bail and Laurie trying to put the cups on her.

Ryan called out with this rhetorical question: 'What do you think you're trying to do, Laurie, get the cream out first?'

An out-of-life experience

Dianne Haworth

The late, colourful New Zealand country singer Kimball Brisco Johnson liked to recount an unexplainable event which, he claimed, once saved his life.

In 1976 while working as a fisherman on the east coast of the North Island, his boat sank and he spent six and a half hours in the sea off the Gisborne coast at Whangara. His strength was going and he feared he was about to drown, when he remembered the words that had once been given to him when he lived in Ruatoria by Sarah Awatere, who Kimball described as being like a tohunga and healer.

Towards the end of her life Sarah had said to him, in acknowledgement of his many kindnesses to her: 'Kimmy, Kimmy, one day you're going to need me. And when you need me you think of the cabbage tree and I'll come.'

Kimball had never thought much about it, but as he was drowning at Whangara he decided to ask Sarah to help him. Although he knew she was dead, he prayed in his head to her: 'Sarah, I'm knackered. If you can help me now I'd appreciate it.'

Kimball would then describe what happened: 'This lone Maori fisherman, Artie Raymond, suddenly appears from nowhere in his little boat and comes and rescues me.

'Something he couldn't explain drove him there,' he later told me. "I don't know why I went there. I'd never fished around those parts before, but as I was going along the coast some very powerful urge made me come here and I found you."

'I've never doubted that my life was saved that day by Sarah.'

Quick off the mark
Ann Pascoe

My grandfather, a well-known farmer of the time, and also well known for his sense of humour and getting a few people's backs up, was attending his small town's livestock sale day.

The big crowd was attentive as a huge bull was ushered into the sales arena, the auctioneer calling out in his usual style, 'And what bids are you going to start me off on for this fine-looking bull? Just look at him, he's hung bigger than George Walter!'

'Aaaah,' my grandfather sighs loudly, but not missing a beat, 'I see your wife's been talking again!'

Turn the bloody thing off!

Don Alman

Having toured the North Island, it came time to go home. We decided to depart from Hamilton and booked into the Airport Motel for two days. The room had a great big spa tub, queen-sized bed and a fancy clock-radio-phone-fax-computer thingy-majig. Not only did we not have a use for it, we hadn't a clue how to turn it on. Settled in, we walked over to the Avis desk and hired a car for two days and were away to see the sights.

That evening at the motel, we filled the spa and enjoyed a refreshing soak, a nice hot cuppa, a biscuit or two, then off to bed.

'What's that?' we said, as we sat bolt upright to a very loud alarm that could have woken the dead. I see that fancy clock-radio, glowing in the dark, push and fiddle every button, but the eardrum-shattering noise continues. I pull its plug, but it still didn't stop. I put it on the bed, threw a pillow over it and lay on top of it with my sixteen stone to smother the thing to death. It didn't seem to make any difference at first, but within a few seconds all went quiet, except for the ringing in our ears.

We lay awake for a while and noticed the other guests who had woken up soon go back to their rooms.

No one knew it was me that made that terrible noise. Very soon we were asleep.

Two hours later, the thing starts making the same bloody noise. 'It must have a battery, pull it out and turn the bloody thing off,' she says. I found it, pulled it out but the noise didn't stop. I threw the thing on the bed, placed a pillow over it and smothered it as before. It worked. Silence.

She said, 'Everyone is up again trying to figure out who has made that noise. Don't turn the light on or make a sound and no one will know it's you.'

We awoke at 8 a.m. By the time we had finished breakfast in our room and dressed, it was 9.45 a.m. I opened the door and found not one car outside. I could walk around without anyone pointing a finger at me about that racket last night.

Into the car and away for another day.

That evening at reception, I said, 'As we are leaving in the morning, could our account be made up so we can pay it after dinner?' After dinner, a few more drinks, then off to reception to pay the bill. Expecting $350 or more on the tab, the bill was less than half this amount.

The receptionist explained. 'No, sir, your account is correct. We offer our sincere apologies; we have discounted your account because the computer for the fire alarm was playing up last night and none of us knew how to turn the bloody thing off.'

Body language

Right up there for Thicko of the Year Award was a young man who had been arrested on suspicion of breaking and entering. He had been taken back to the station for questioning, but the interview was not progressing smoothly, however — they could not even get the man to acknowledge that his name was 'John'.

'C'mon, we know your name's John — let's just move on, eh?' the interviewing sergeant said for what must have been about the seventh time.

''Snot John!'

'C'mon, John. Admit it. We know! Then we can move on and clear this whole matter up,' coaxed the sergeant, fighting hard to conceal his exasperation.

''*Snot* John!'

'Then why, mate, do you have J-O-H-N tattooed to your forehead?'

Karma the kahu
Debbie Stewart

I've been a falconer since the 1980s with a particular passion for New Zealand's falcons and hawks. The sport — indeed, the 'art' of falconry — has a rich history and culture reaching back to China around

2000 BC. But in this country, apart from the old stories of Kurungaitutu, and Pouakai (the large but now extinct eagle), birds of prey have rarely featured in myth and legend.

Today, falconry in New Zealand is practised by a limited number of enthusiasts, and the purpose and focus of the training techniques have changed. Essentially, the training of the birds is to prepare them for release into the wild and this might include the training of the harrier hawk, kahu, or the New Zealand falcon, karearea.

Some time ago I had taken in a young female harrier hawk. She was the only surviving eyas found by farmers during haymaking and I named her Karma. She was an amazing bird. Large enough to be intimidating — almost a metre in wingspan — with dark chocolate brown in plumage, and deep, dark, black eyes you could swim in. She was totally mesmerising and absorbing. At just over a month old, she learned quickly and within four days I could call her for titbits to the glove. She was free-flying!

Over some months, our daily training sessions were intensive and regular. Each day I would feed her, fly her, and return her to the aviary at night. Just one problem remained. Unlike her wild counterparts that soared the skies with complete abandonment, Karma would fly readily to the glove but appeared to have no sense at all of the available airspace above. She would only fly the height of the held-out hand and glove — one and a half metres from the ground. Karma, with all of her grandeur, appeared to be afraid of heights.

In an attempt to combat the problem, I literally tried to 'throw' her off a mountain. Mt Ngongotaha in Rotorua was the perfect choice — the thermals and lift offered by the upwinds would provide an excellent learning curve.

I walked Karma sitting on my gloved hand from the lower slopes of the Paradise Valley hills to the tops of the mountain. It was a steep climb. Puffing, I was thrilled to reach the summit. What could be better? I launched her, rather ungainly, but full of expectation, from the top of the mountain. As she circled the available thermal I attempted to call her with my whistle to return. A simple circle of flight was all I expected.

Unfortunately, while she did 'circle', it was a flight I did not anticipate. She spiralled all the way down to the foot of the mountain. I blew the whistle, and she landed on the ground. I blew the whistle again, and in an effort to be responsive, she promptly started *walking* back up the mountain! Unless I could magically grow wings and show her how to fly, this was going to be a major problem.

I gave it further thought and figured the best chance would be the sea breeze thermals offered by the east coast. I packed the car, packed the bird, and headed for the sea.

Ohope beach was the first choice. Relatively quiet, good sea breezes, and the coast marked by huge steep cliff faces for good lift. Not least the dramatic Christmas flowering of pohutukawa for added artistic ambience. After checking in at the local camp spot —

not as easy as one might imagine with a hawk tethered in the front seat of the car — we settled quickly, fed, rested, and slept in anticipation of the following day's flight.

Early morning, and the weather was perfect. We managed to escape the fellow campers without drawing attention and headed for the beach. Falconry tends to be a solitary event; training of the birds means we generally avoid distractions, so we found a stretch of beach with few people.

Unfortunately nobody told the seagulls. Within metres of stepping onto the beach, I swear hundreds of gulls appeared from nowhere. They instantly recognised Karma as their predator. It was obvious we needed to find somewhere else to work.

Just when I was about to think that this was a really dumb idea I spied a small picnic reserve just off the beach. Perfect! No people, no dogs, no seagulls. Just me and Karma.

I slipped her leash. I removed her jesses. She launched into the air and within seconds must have been some fifty metres above. The thermals worked! I was elated! I called her with the whistle and a small titbit of meat to the glove. Her wings pulled in, and almost stalled in the wind, she slowly lost altitude and returned to the glove for her reward. It was a major development: she had wind, she had control. I launched her and she was soaring. Karma was striding the skies. I was thrilled; I danced, and I laughed out loud.

Karma enjoyed it too. It was obvious, as I watched her flights silhouetted against the Ohope cliff faces.

She circled, she soared, she thermalled. For the first time she did indeed fly like an eagle. My kahu — I was so very proud.

After about half an hour of watching her newfound vigour for flying, I figured it was time to call her back to the glove. But she was in no hurry. She took her time. Karma either had a fresh enthusiasm for her new skills, couldn't see me, or was out of earshot. I blew the whistle repeatedly in frustration. I blew it louder. Nothing worked.

In the meantime, a local family turned up at the picnic area. I tried to be nonchalant sitting on the park bench while they went through their preparation rituals of picnic blankets and setting up for lunch.

I wasn't ready for big explanations of the what, why and wherefore of what I was doing. The family equally kept to themselves. As time went on, I was becoming increasingly concerned about Karma. I knew she was well trained, but she didn't know the area. I started to worry. I blew the whistle repeatedly. I brought out additional food for her, little morsels she couldn't resist, and laid them on the park bench around me.

I started to draw attention to myself, and could see the father of the family throwing me repeated anxious glances. I blew the whistle, I put my glove in the air, I hit my hand, and I put more titbits out in full view. Eventually, no longer able to resist the questions, the father came over. I saw him coming but I was increasingly concerned and anxious about Karma.

'Are you OK?' he asked as he approached. This seemed a major understatement. Here I was blowing my whistle, wearing full leathers in the height of summer, looking skywards, and surrounded by dead chickens.

By this time, I wasn't in the best of moods, so without huge explanations figured that it best to keep it short. 'Yeah, just waiting for my bird,' I replied. He looked at me, my glove, and the dead chickens, then slowly nodded as if he understood, backed away very slowly and returned to his family. Within minutes, their picnic was packed, they got in the car, and left.

It didn't worry me particularly at the time. I was relieved just to know the picnic area was mine again, but within ten minutes the police arrived. I remained blowing my whistle, hitting my glove, looking skywards, with dead chickens all around. Strangely enough the policeman asked the same question.

I thought I'd better give him a bit more information. 'Yep, I'm fine — I'm just waiting for my hawk.' I looked skywards and tried to point out Karma. I don't think he believed me, but he seemed satisfied I wasn't a risk to anyone, and he also left.

Within minutes of the police leaving, Karma must have seen the opportunity to return without distraction or interruptions. She pulled her wings in tight, almost stooping like a falcon, and alighted to the glove. She ate well, but vocalised loudly in between morsels as though she was excited by the flight. She was hyped. I was hyped. I looked around hoping for vindication, but no one remained as a witness.

Life as a falconer has its moments.

Laurie and the lizard

For those of you who remember six o'clock in the public bars, you will know what a rush it used to be to get to the pub after work and to down as many jugs of beer as you could before being thrown out onto the streets right on six.

Now Laurie was no exception. He used to rush to the pub every night after work for the six o'clock swill along with all his mates. Laurie was a big fellow, about six foot tall and 130 kg in weight. He loved his wife and kids as much as his beer. He owned bulldozers and a large transporter truck, which suited his big and happy personality.

This story begins one Saturday when it was raining cats and dogs and Laurie headed to the pub early afternoon and proceeded to get himself nicely plastered along with several of his mates. They all sat around a large table and told yarns and laughed and smoked without a care in the world.

At five o'clock Laurie's other great mate Morris arrived from work to have a beer. Morris was also a big bloke and he owned a business of front-end loaders. On this Saturday he had been clearing up an old wool-scouring factory which had had a fire during the week and all of the burnt dags had to be dumped. Morris grabbed himself a jug and a handle of beer and bought one for Laurie and they sat next to each other and started to catch up on the events of the day.

Morris suddenly remembered that he had caught a lizard in amongst the rubbish and he had put it in the top pocket of his overalls to take home for his kids. Seeing that Laurie was well on the way he decided to have a joke, so he carefully placed the lizard into Laurie's half-full handle of beer without Laurie seeing him.

Morris watched Laurie carefully to see what his reaction would be. He was not disappointed. By the time Laurie had picked up his handle, the poor old lizard had struggled out of the beer bath and was just starting to crawl up over the rim of the handle. When Laurie had the handle up to his mouth he saw the lizard eyeballing him at close range.

'Jesus Christ,' yelled Laurie, and the handle of beer went flying straight up into the air. Laurie fell backwards, chair and all, and his huge legs kicked the table over along with jugs of beer, handles of beer and human, drunk bodies, all of which ended in a crumpled wet mess on the carpeted floor.

The bar manager was not amused and as it was near enough to six o'clock, he ordered the whole gang out of the bar and onto the street. They all stood around and tried to talk Laurie out of driving his old Bedford truck home, but Laurie was not having any of that rubbish.

'I'm as sober as a judge.'

They watched him disappear over the rail line and along the road to his house which was quite close.

Now, the road Laurie lived in was quite narrow and there was a deep drain alongside which had culvert pipes and fill to form each house entrance, but not very wide. Inevitably, Laurie managed to put the front of the Bedford over the edge of the culvert, so he was stranded on his own drive entrance.

Laurie inspected the situation, hands on hips and rocking backwards and forwards, and decided he would phone his driver, who had also been at the pub, to bring the transporter with the D4 bulldozer around and they would tow the Bedford out.

The idea was good so far, but Laurie decided to drive the dozer off the side of the transporter rather than struggle with the heavy tail ramp. This was a fatal error. The little dozer went off the side of the transporter on an acute angle and it too ended up stranded nearly on its side, jammed against the truck and unable to move clear.

By this time a sizeable crowd had started to gather in the street to watch the circus. Then Mr Whippy's truck also appeared on the scene and there were kids all over the place. What a performance!

Laurie's wife by this time had started to panic and had phoned Laurie's brother with the logging truck to come to her rescue. The brother was sober so he took control and soon had the transporter and the bulldozer sorted. He then towed the Bedford back onto the road and very soon all was well.

As a consequence of this performance, and with pressure from his wife, Laurie made a pledge to get off the booze.

His best mate, Des, had a bet with him for $200 that he could outlast Laurie on the wagon no trouble at all, so they both agreed that the first one to start drinking owed the other $200.

For weeks after the bet Laurie would go to the bar and drink a couple of handles of lemonade, usually with Des, and he would always go home early with a long face and stone-cold sober. He even started mowing the lawns each week, and his wife started to get sick of him moping around the house so she made him peel spuds and vacuum the house.

One Monday after work Laurie arrived at the pub minus his eyebrows and with his front hair missing from his head. When questioned he said his bully had caught fire and he got singed. Yeah right!

Anyhow, he and Des had lasted a month off the booze so they both shook hands in front of their mates and agreed that no one had won the bet and they would start to drink again with no money passing hands.

What a party that session was. Laurie's wife was probably thankful that the bet was over also.

Some time later, Laurie finally admitted what had happened to his hair and eyebrows. He and Des had got so sick of not drinking that they had decided to go away whitebaiting. The trip was to include a barbecue alongside the river so they purchased some sausages and, as they were out of town, two dozen large bottles of beer to wash them down.

Of course, temptation got the better of them once they had their nets in the water, so they started on the booze.

A couple of hours later, when the booze was nearly finished, and they had caught no whitebait, they decided that a sausage might go down well. They collected some driftwood to light a fire and were going to cook the sausages on a shovel. Unfortunately, the fire would not start, so Laurie grabbed a can of chainsaw fuel from the Bedford, leant over the smouldering wood and poured the petrol onto it.

The rest is history. The hair and eyebrows disappeared in a flash.

Home brew

Paulene Lowe

Times were pretty tough during the war years for most families and ours was no exception, what with Mum, Dad and five kids to feed.

My dad always loved his beer, so he took to making his first home-brew. I believe it was a potent brew and we were forbidden to go into the back shed, as Dad would bravely enter each day to check how many bottles had exploded.

Six to eight weeks later the big tasting took place, with lots of friends invited to share the brew. There was great excitement as Dad poured everyone a drink and one for himself and Mum. As everybody took a sip, a deathly silence descended and then someone mentioned mothballs, then another, then another.

Apparently in those days, at some stage you had to strain the brew. Mum had got out one of the clean blankets for the process, forgetting that she had stored the blankets in mothballs.

No one seemed to mind the mothballs taste as every last bottle was opened and drunk. I remember there were some massive headaches, but everyone lived to a ripe old age and kept coming to visit our home.

One-eyed Pete

Pete was a renowned shearer and a determined drinker, and he'd signed on with a shearing crew way up bush. He had to catch the 5 a.m. mail train to get there, so he booked into the local Railway Hotel.

Thinking a drink wouldn't hurt, he got stuck into the grog with a few mates. When he finally retired to catch a couple of hours' sleep, his drinking mates thought they would play a trick on Pete, so they crept into his room and shaved off one of his bushy eyebrows.

The publican shook him awake at 4 a.m. and Pete staggered to the washroom, where he gaped at his face and screamed: 'Oh Christ! They've woken the wrong bloody man!'

And finally, rest assured the future of yarn-telling in New Zealand is in good hands. The following story is from our youngest contributor, eight-year-old Kushla Kozeluh.

The pink bats

Kushla Kozeluh

'Grandma,' said Kushla, 'have you ever been bitten by a pink bat?'

'A pink bat?' Grandma looked puzzled. 'Tell me a bit more about these pink bats.'

'Well, they live in the ceilings of houses, lots and lots of them, and if you get bitten they leave bits of glass in your fingers. Have *you* ever been bitten?'

'Aaah!' said Grandma. 'I think you might be talking about *Pink Batts*!'

Tony piped up from his chair in the corner, 'We've got lots of Pink Batts right here, but they are spelt with two 't's and they don't fly around. Would you like to see them? I've got a big ladder and we can lift out that square in the ceiling and have a look if you like.'

(Tony is Grandma's husband and so really the grandkids' grandpoppy. Mostly Kushla calls him Tony, but sometimes TonyPonyMacaroni and sometimes TonyCuppaTea because he's always making cups of tea.)

Kushla shrank back. 'No way! I'm not going up there!'

Tony went and got the ladder even though Kushla was still shaking her head firmly. He was talking about how the heat has to stay *out* of the house in the summer and the warmth has to stay *inside* the house in the winter. Grandma says he always explains a bit more than you really want to know.

Tony put the ladder up and moved the square in the ceiling. It looked very dark up in that hole. Grandma got a torch and climbed carefully up the ladder. 'Kushla,' she called, 'here are the Pink Batts. I think you can just see the edge of some from down there. I'll come down and we can climb up together if you like.'

'I'm not going up there,' Kushla said firmly.

Grandma was a bit wicked then. 'I bet if Gino was here he would be up that ladder like a shot.' Gino is Kushla's cousin. He's two years younger, only five, but he's always doing things that Grandma says are 'rash'.

After a little bit more egging on, Kushla went slowly up the ladder, with Grandma one rung behind. She peeked nervously in to see the Pink Batts. And the spiderwebs! Yuck!

Kushla hung out bravely at the top of the ladder for a few minutes before scuttling back down to ground level. She and Grandma and Tony compared their attic with all the other attics in Kushla's great imagination. They concluded that this one was a bit of a disappointment and so were the Pink Batts — they were pretty boring and more grubby than pink. Then Tony put the ceiling back the way it usually was.

Later that day Auntie Eve visited with Gino and

little Leo. Everybody stood out by the cars talking. After a few minutes Gino and Kushla went down to the house; standing around while grown-ups yak on gets awfully boring. When Grandma came down five minutes later she found Kushla and Gino standing under the square in the ceiling.

'Kushla says there's a hole in the roof, Grandma. She says she went up there on a big ladder. She did not, did she, Grandma?'

'Well, actually,' said Grandma casually, 'she did.'

'Freeeeeaky!' said Gino with big, wide eyes. 'No way *I* want to go into that hole!'

'Maybe I'll just bring in the ladder again and Kushla can show you,' said Grandma slyly.

She put the ladder up again and moved the square of ceiling. Quick as a flash, Kushla climbed the ladder. 'See, Gino, it's not scary at all! It's easy peasy!'

She climbed back down, looking very pleased with herself, and gave Gino the very kind, generous encouragement that only an older cousin can. 'Try it. You'll be OK. I'll climb behind you if you're scared,' she said.

'OK,' said Gino, reluctantly. He slowly climbed, step by step, making sure Kushla was close behind. 'Freaky!' he said when they got to the top. 'I want to go down now.'

'I've never climbed up there before either. I was a bit scared too,' Grandma confessed later, smiling to see how very, very pleased Kushla was with herself.

War stories

The military was full of humour but at the same time full of discipline. One of the problems with military humour is that it is almost necessary to have served in the armed forces to understand many of the attitudes which consider something to be humorous and another thing, quite similar, to be depressing.

Jokes varied according to the success or failure experienced while on operations. If a Wing suffered heavy losses the humour seemed to develop an atmosphere bordering on the macabre, while the high spirits induced by victories gave rise to frivolity and carefree attitudes.

Every squadron had a prankster. Most of my comrades were genial, likeable and always ready for a joke.

Jack Stafford

War ditties

**Remembered by
Jack Stafford**

The Young British Airman

Oh, the young British Airman lay dying
And as in the wreckage he lay
To his comrades gathered around him
These last dying words he did say.

Take the cylinder out of my kidney
The connecting rod out from my brain

From the small of my back take the crankshaft
And assemble the engine again.

Wrap me up in my old flying jacket
And say a poor pilot lies low
Have six stalwart comrades to carry me
With steps solemn, mournful and slow.

When the Court of Inquiry assembled
To find out the reason he died
'Twas a flat spin which closely resembled
The maximum angle of glide.

Now stand by your glasses steady,
This world is a world full of lies.
Here's a toast to the dead already
And here's to the next one that dies.

A slightly macabre version of 'The Young British Airman' was also popular when appropriate:

I'll be out on the clouds in the morning
With the sun shining bright in my eyes
And my wings are softly sighing
Hooray for the next man to die.

So stand by your glasses steady
Here's a toast to the man in the skies
Here's good luck to the dead already
And here's to the next man to die.

When I was on 80 Squadron RAF, one of the pilots had a relative who had flown during the First World War. He taught him this. We sang it but he only knew the one verse:

> Back safe at the airfield, feeling brave and bright
> We'll take a car to Amiens, have dinner there
>   tonight,
> We'll stroll along the boulevards and meet the girls
>   of France
> To hell with Army medical, we'll take our bloody
>   chance.

Kiwis on parade

Maurice Flahive

On a June day in 1946 I was in the first draft of NZEF Japan, otherwise known as J Force, and we'd just arrived in Japan. We were hanging over the side of the ship, keen for our first sight of the 'enemy', the people who'd just waged a bloody and ferocious war on our Pacific world.

Our ship came alongside the wharf at Kure and we had our first look at them — wharfies, all men of military age, most of them dressed in military surplus gear. I turned to my mates nearby and asked, 'Well, what do you think of them?'

A chorus came back, 'They all look the bloody same, mate!'

As a signalman I was attached to 27 Battalion at Yamaguchi City before I was transferred down to Hagi with my good mate Colin.

Around 9.30 one evening I answered an incoming call from a very agitated Mommasan. I caught the words 'New Zearando Sordiers' and 'MPs'. In the background I could hear laughter and the sound of things breaking. I tried to convince her to call the Japanese police but she was screaming by now and wanting MPs, MPs!

The duty sergeant and an interpreter sped down-town in a jeep, but were too late to catch the two Kiwi 'terrorists' who'd been causing all the trouble. They must have known a good shortcut back to camp because every one of the company was present and correct at curfew time.

Next morning the order came that every person in camp who wasn't on essential duty was to be on parade. When we'd formed two long lines Major Palmer, the CO, and the interpreter arrived with a very nervous-looking Mommasan. There must have been two very nervous blokes on parade — this was a line-up! Poor old Mommasan. She slowly walked the full length of the lines, looking into every face, then heaved a huge sigh and said something to the interpreter.

We were all ordered to remove our berets and she walked past us all once more. She stopped halfway, spoke to the interpreter and then walked forward and put her hand on my shoulder.

I don't think we saw Major Palmer smile too often

but I was very relieved to see his knowing grin behind Mommasan, as she was told that I was the one who had answered her call on the switchboard the night before so it couldn't have been me.

We were stood down and poor old Mommasan turned and said something to the interpreter. I asked him later what she had said. It was the Japanese equivalent of:

They all look the bloody same, mate!

Watch my arse

Jack Stafford

The sabre engine in the Typhoon roared. I watched Woe sitting in the other kite. He signalled to me, released his brakes and the aircraft started to move forward from the dispersal. As he taxied along the perimeter track, his speed increased and he moved swiftly towards the western end of the airfield.

Feeling tense but more than ready to do the job in hand, I followed.

* * *

The winter day was grey and cold. Low cloud swept across the airfield and the pilots sat around the little stoves in the dispersals smoking, playing cards and waiting. A quarter of an hour earlier I had been sitting with them when the Flight Commander, Frank Murphy, walked in. 'Wilson, take Stafford and carry out a patrol along the French Coast from Boulogne to Dieppe. Some Spits went out to do a rhubarb a while ago and they have been playing hide and seek with some Hun fighters in the cloud. They should be coming out from France soon. You provide a bit of support in case they are intercepted. Have a look in all the harbours as you go down the coast for anything unusual in the shipping.' Frank looked at me. 'Ready for your first show, Staff?'

'Yes, sir,' I answered, my excitement rising. On operations at last. This was the culmination of all the training, all the waiting, all the hoping for acceptance, all the fear of rejection. Back from this and I would be an operational pilot.

Woe Wilson had been on the squadron for some time and had shown me consideration and friendship since my arrival a month or so earlier. I was glad it was him I was going with. Frank Murphy was a most able and astute leader. He knew I'd be comfortable and well looked after, flying with Woe.

We picked up our Mae Wests and, with our parachutes, we moved out to the aircraft.

'Keep up with me, Staff,' said Woe. 'Don't lag or stuff around. I'll be busy enough without looking after you.'

I nodded and then said, 'Any particular instructions?'

'Yes,' said Woe. 'Remember you're only here to make sure we don't get bounced by some cunning little Huns in their dangerous Focke-Wulfs or 109s. Just watch my arse.'

We walked on in silence each deep in our own thoughts.

* * *

The green light flashed at us from the control tower. We moved onto the runway and turned into wind. Woe looked across, his face obscured by the oxygen mask. He gave me the thumbs up and turned his head back. I saw him opening up and I did the same. Side by side we thundered down the runway with breathtaking acceleration. Smoothly we left the ground, raised our undercarts and climbed away into that overcast, threatening sky. I throttled back to stay with Woe and checked the airspeed indicator, 190 mph — we were climbing steadily. Tangmere disappeared into the gloom behind us as we scuttled across the countryside. We crossed the coast and dropped swiftly to low level just above the waves. We went into cruise mode, 3600 rpm, +4½ boost. Woe set course for France. I scanned the sky above and behind. Watching, always watching.

It seemed no time till Woe called me up.

'OK, Music Red 2, climbing now to just below cloud base. Enemy coast ahead.' Our Typhoons lifted and the coast of France appeared. I took a quick glance then swivelled my neck around, searching the sky above and behind Woe's rudder.

We almost reached the coastal sands when Woe called again. '90 degrees starboard, Red 2.' We turned and started down the coast. At each port we swung low over the roadstead and I would risk a quick look at the shipping below and the harbour buildings. It was all new to me. Then I would swiftly scan the sky; a sky that may hold a dozen FW190s looking for us or the returning Spits. At each new spot on my windshield or each imagined shadow in the clouds my pulse sped up. So we droned on towards Dieppe, continuing to dutifully carry out our instructions.

My earphones crackled and control's voice came through. 'Music aircraft, Kenway calling, are you receiving me, over?'

'Hello, Kenway, Music Red 1 receiving you loud and clear,' said Woe.

'Return to base all Music aircraft. Repeat, return to base. Kenway out.'

'Roger Wilco, out,' said Woe. Again my earphones crackled and Woe's voice spoke. 'Spits must be home,' he said to me. 'Turning starboard onto 320 degrees.'

Smoothly we turned and started back across the Channel. The cruel, indifferent, sullen, turbulent, all-devouring Channel. This stretch of sea that was the last resting place for so many warrior airmen. We flew back close under the cloud, ready to use it as a refuge if a squadron of Hun fighters appeared out of the mist.

Woe watched his heading. I watched Woe's tail.

'Turn on your IFF, Staff. England coming up,' Woe's voice broke through the Typhoon's drone. I threw the switch 'Identification Friend or Foe'. This was a necessity to protect us from our own flak and perhaps our own patrolling fighters. No fighters in this weather, I thought.

The cloud base lowered and we crossed the English coast almost on the deck, slightly west of Brighton. Woe knew every inch of the south coast and soon we swung low over Chichester, and the Tangmere runway came into view.

The call came. 'Echelon starboard, Red 2.' We roared along the downwind leg. Crosswind, lower undercarriage, green lights on. Flaps down and the Typhoon changed attitude. We approached at about 130 mph, crossed the perimeter track, pulled back on the stick gently and dropped like two feathers side by side onto the runway. Woe looked across at me and nodded. I felt that he was pleased. We kept a bit of throttle on and sped down the runway towards the 486 Squadron dispersal. We slowed to walking pace as the ground crew came into view waving us into our parking sites.

I came to a halt and switched her off. The grinning mechanic was up on the wing as I wound back the hood. Still smiling he helped me with the straps.

'How did the first op go?'

I grinned back at him even wider. 'Just great,' I said.

'Did you get a Hun?' he laughed.

'No such luck, never even saw one,' I said.

He patted my shoulder. 'You will!'

Woe was waiting for me and we walked together to the dispersal. 'Good show, Staff,' he said, and he smiled. I felt warm at this unusual praise. I couldn't stop grinning.

All flying had been cancelled because of the weather. It had clagged right down. We entered the dispersal to find it jammed tight with pilots. Another Typhoon Squadron at Tangmere was paying us a visit, taking advantage of the duff conditions. All heads turned as we entered. All knew it was my first 'op'. Frank Murphy was standing at the door to greet us and he shook my hand enthusiastically.

He said to Woe, 'How did it go?'

'Good,' said Woe. 'Piece of cake.' The intelligence officer stepped up and spoke to Woe. The noise died down in the room.

'What did you see, Woe?'

'Several ships in the port at Le Treport, one leaving the roadstead. Bit of movement around Boulogne but most of the shipping was at Dieppe.'

'Did you get much flak?'

'Yes, quite a bit,' said Woe. 'Dieppe was the heaviest and they hosed us a bit from all the other ports. Even got a bit from the coast.'

I stood there locked in amazement, my mouth open. Flak! What bloody flak?

The CO of the visiting squadron must have noticed my obvious confusion and asked 'Did you see the flak, Staff?'

I faced him, my mouth dry. Almost inaudibly I answered, 'No.'

He was smiling at me, and at my answer he started to laugh. Gales of good-natured laughter rocked the room. The goodwill towards me and my ready acceptance by all was obvious and infectious. Murph was killing himself laughing. He put a hand on my shoulder and said, 'Staff, you're a bloody beaut.'

Without knowing what we were laughing about I joined in too. Woe laughed, the IO laughed, everybody was in fits.

Woe said, 'He was watching my arse and doing it well.' For no reason this produced more screams of laughter. It was all just hilarious.

At that moment a ground staff man approached the dispersal. Murph went out to meet him. He came back with a jagged piece of steel in his hand.

It was three to four inches long and all edges and points, grey-black in colour and looked murderous, sinister, pitiless.

'This was just removed from your aircraft's spinner, Staff,' he said quietly and handed it to me. I took it silently and studied it. A chunk of spent German flak.

'Wouldn't look too good in your eye for a wart, Staff,' said a pilot. This initiated another dozen smart remarks, most offering other possibilities as to where else it could have been stuck. The laughter was away again. My jaw ached, my sides ached. Everything seemed so funny . . .

With all the squadrons stood down, slowly everyone drifted away to the mess.

I was swollen with pride. I felt I was a fighter pilot. Not much of a fighter pilot but still a fighter pilot. Sure it was only the smallest of small shows but we had intruded into enemy-occupied airspace.

It was the first step in my operational career. I was a fighter pilot in 486 Fighter Squadron 11 Group Fighter Command Tangmere. Sure I was proud.

We went into the mess. I shouted. Everybody

shouted me. We ate. I drank too much. We left the station in a couple of cars.

'Off to the Ship,' came the cry, as we left for this favourite watering hole in Chichester. It was a lost night but I remember how it started, even now.

I treasured that piece of flak for many months. The war dragged on; the combat became grim and grimmer as the months passed. Such souvenirs lost their importance as life became more insecure and precarious.

I lost the piece of flak.

Good things take time

Jack Stafford

Western Desert, 1942. New Zealand soldiers receive mail. Great excitement. There is a general ripping open of envelopes and sad faces, happy faces and silent men who look into the distance.

One guy not considered an Einstein or bright in any way shouted with glee as he danced around.

His only close friend, Charlie, smilingly said, 'What is it, Bob, what's your news?'

'My wife is having a baby,' said Bob, with a face like a summer morning.

Charlie's expression changed to wonderment as he softly said, 'Hey, Bob, mate, we've been here in the desert for eighteen months. That's a long time.'

'I know, I know,' Bob answered. 'She took two years after we were married to have the first one.'

Korean hopsicles

Dudley C Pye

During the Christmas of 1953 I was a young soldier/ cook serving in Korea. The practice of the government was to issue soldiers with a beer ration on days such as Christmas Day, Anzac Day, and so on.

Two bottles of lager were issued per soldier for Christmas Day; they were to be consumed with lunch in an effort to improve morale.

The intense cold (minus fifteen degrees centigrade) caused the beer to become somewhat frozen and great difficulty was experienced in attempting to consume the much anticipated brew.

As it was so cold, many soldiers were gathered around my field stove and some bottles were placed on top of the range where the bottoms became heated a little. Soon the heat began to force the beer up through the neck of the bottles like a candle-shaped periscope.

The soldiers then proceeded to chew lumps from the beer candles as they rose from the bottle like some kind of hopsicle. As the beer warmed too much, the bottle was placed in the snow to refreeze and the process was repeated.

What a Christmas! And those memories are recalled each Anzac Day as the tastiest Christmas candles ever invented.

This now old cook still likes a cold drop on a hot day.

Shelter of the Good Shepherd

Jack Stafford

I was at a bar in Halifax, Yorkshire, with another pilot when we were joined by another couple of pilots, known to my companion Tony. He greeted them warmly. We all talked for a while then Tony asked them what they had been up to. One said, 'We've been to Ireland on leave.'

We asked how and why, so we came to hear this story.

'Well,' said Spotty, the freckled one, 'we were flying Hurricanes from an airfield near Liverpool, doing convoy patrols over the Irish Sea, a very boring job. Three of us were just stooging around, bored to death, when out of the cloud dived a couple of Ju88s which attacked the convoy. One unloaded his bombs and scarpered for the cloud cover when he saw us turn onto them but the other pilot must have been after an Iron Cross as he forced on regardless, attacking the freighter he had singled out and had in his sights.' Spotty paused. 'You remember Shorty Robinson?'

'Yes' said Tony. 'Wasn't he the smartarse who made a joke of everything?'

'He was,' said Spotty, 'but he was also very determined when he met the Hun. He was not at all funny then. Shorty fastened onto the arse of the 88 and poured the lead into him and one of his engines began to smoke. His Ju88 began to lose height and the pilot turned and headed for Ireland, the south part, but his gunner never stopped pouring it back at Shorty as they went down. He hit Shorty with a good burst and the Hurricane began to smoke badly. He was just as pig-headed as the Hun and stuck to his arse, shooting like hell. You could have walked on the lead that was being fired between them.

'All at once the Hun faltered and fell, one guy jumped and his parachute opened; we thought it was the pilot as we felt the gunner was probably dead. Shorty called up and said he was wounded and he couldn't make it back to England or even to the convoy and so was going to try to bail out as close to shore as he could get. He did but we didn't go too close for a look as we thought those Micky Doolan boys might have a few ack-ack guns trained on us. He looked pretty close in to land to us as he hit the water of the Irish Sea and we were confident that the Irish police would pick him up. We flew back to Liverpool put in a claim for one destroyed on behalf of Shorty and that was that.

'A couple of weeks later I had a letter from Shorty; he was in a hospital in Dublin. He reckoned he was there for the duration, until the war ended. He had quite a few wounds and in addition he had become very friendly with a most salubrious little nurse the like of which he hadn't often met. Also, the Irish had interned him.'

'The bastards,' said Tony, 'they've buried him.'

'Interned, not interred, you dumb prick,' answered

Spotty. I heard later that he had had to look it up in the dictionary himself. 'Anyway, Shorty said the games that he and the nurse were playing beat hell out of chasing Huns. He was in no hurry to leave but he missed the companionship of his fellow pilots and wanted me to visit. He reckoned we'd have a lot of fun.

'I didn't think it was possible but talked it over with the Adjutant. He said he would put in an application for me and Mick. He did. You had to have Irish relatives living there — and you remember Brian Brennan? Had hundreds of Irish relatives. He was on our squadron and he had to swear that we were cousins, blood cousins.'

Tony said, 'That would have cost him a couple of hundred Our Fathers.'

Spotty ignored him and went on. 'We borrowed some mufti, got our tickets and we were there. We had a couple of great days in Dublin then settled down and began to look for Shorty. I knew the name of the hospital, which was the Shelter of the Good Shepherd, but had no idea where it was. We were wandering down O'Connell Street and I saw this tough-looking Irish cop. Very politely I inquired as to his health and he assured me it was perfect. Having broken the ice I explained our situation.

'Well, now it's from New Zealand that you've come, is it? And could it be that a little bit of the blood of the Irish runs in your veins and gives you that freckled face and the touch of ginger in your hair?'

I gave him a friendly non-committal smile, as I didn't want any depth to his inquiry.

'And it's the Shelter of the Good Shepherd where you'll be looking for your friend?'

'Yes,' I said. 'I felt that you would know.'

'Well,' says the cop, 'it's in O'Connell Street you'll find yourself now, the most beautiful street in the most beautiful city in Europe. Dublin is the toast of the world, and the brains of the world have begun their lives here. We've James, Yeats, Shaw, Wilde and hundreds more. Now you're sure it's to see your friend you'll be looking?'

I nodded.

'Look you there and you see the statue to that great Irish patriot Charles Stewart Parnell? Be doffing your caps as you pass it. A couple of blocks on and a right turn you should make and before you, only a street or two away stands the wonder of the Christian faith, the Cathedral of the Sacred Heart. Go in there, my boys, kneel and repent, confess your sins and cleanse your souls. Stay awhile and remember your sorrows. On your way out make use of the holy water and make a generous donation to the poor in the box provided. It's buoyant you'll be feeling as you walk away with fresh life in your step.

'Down the road continue for a few blocks and what the Hell is this, you'll be saying to yerselfs! You'll be seeing a strange and ugly building. Holy Mother of God, it's a fish market, you'll be saying! But now as you get closer you'll see it is (the policeman turned and spat on the pavement) the Protestant Church! Ignore it and while clasping your nostrils quickly move on around the corner, Francis Street it could be.

'Now you're entering the joy of Dublin, with its bars and grill shops. Steaks and beer such as you've never tasted in England. Guinness is great, Kilkenny is greater and the steak will in your mouth be melting. It's heaven, you'll be saying. A drop or two of Jamieson's will set you in the mood for fun. It's like kings you'll be treated and around six o'clock the working boys will be coming in and settling for the evening. Eating and drinking they'll be doing and as the evening wears on they'll be singing, telling jokes and enjoying each other. Dancing will start and everyone will be in high spirits. At this point jump both of you onto the table and scream for quiet and as the silence falls, shout out loud "God bless King George and Stuff the Pope."

'When you wake, my bonny boys, you'll find that it's the Shelter of the Good Shepherd you're lying in.'

High and mighty

Jack Stafford

A pompous Wing Commander was sitting in a barber's chair giving orders to the station barber in a most officious voice.

A young Kiwi Flying Officer came in and sat in the next empty chair. 'Good morning, sir,' he said.

There was no reply.

The Wing Commander continued to issue orders to the barber. 'Not there, man! Over on the left,' and so on and so on.

The barber finished and picked up a jar of hair oil. He moved to put it on the Wing Commander's hair.

'Not that damn stuff, barber. For God's sake, my wife will say I smell like a bloody French brothel.'

The young Kiwi said, 'You can put it on me, barber. My wife doesn't know what a French brothel smells like.'

Hunting tales

Rabbit pie

Chris Humphreys

Fiordland. A small word for such a big place.

Three million acres of granite cliffs, ice, jungle, sandflies and water. Hard country. Breeds some hard people too.

Old Nor'wester Jack is one of the hard breed. He came to work on the power station in the sixties and drove a dozer on the Wilmot Pass road until it rolled on him and shattered his shoulder. That kept him off work for a fortnight. The foreman wouldn't let him back on site until he'd taken at least six weeks off so Jack threw the job in and got what he called a 'cushy number' running one of the fast launches across Lake Manapouri to the power house.

Jack loved it on the launches. Especially in the rough weather. Passengers would be strewn all over the boat, groaning and being sick and Jack would be up at the helm laughing at them while keeping a weather-eye on the screaming nor'wester and the pattern of white-capped swells relentlessly rolling in from under the flashes of dancing lightning on the far side of the lake.

Then the project finished, the giant power-house generators gradually hummed into life and the people drifted away. A few stayed on and farmed the bush edges or hunted venison or drove buses and other machinery for the tourists or the Works or the Lands and Survey.

Jack retired. It was 1971 and Jack reckoned he had done enough even though he was only in his mid-fifties. He'd seen North Africa in the war, mustered the Canterbury high country and milled the rimu forests of the West Coast. He'd worked the mines in Australia and done his time on the deep-sea trawlers off Patagonia, although he probably wouldn't think that it was worth mentioning. His body was worn and it showed. He reckoned he needed a rest.

That's not to say that he gave up work. Jack would do the odd day here and there, a lambing beat on one of the Lands and Survey blocks, the occasional bit of tractor driving or cutting a bit of firewood to sell on the side.

Jack had been warned that he was going to be kicked out of his hut in the hydro village. He wasn't worried though; he'd made other arrangements in the form of a rusted twelve-foot Starliner two-berth caravan that was parked down in the manuka on the lakefront. It was rough — it looked a fire had gone through the kitchen at some time in the recent past and the axle assembly was a distant memory. Jack had bought it for two dozen big bottles of beer and a set of Ministry of Works jumper leads that he'd 'borrowed' a few years back.

'Nothin' wrong with it' was Jack's reply when a local asked him about the gorse growing up through the floor.

No one really knows how Jack got his caravan three miles around the shore to a bush terrace overlooking where the river empties into the lake. There was a rumour that Jack had filled the caravan with empty 20-litre drench containers and floated it around behind his dinghy, and then towed it up the bank with a hand-winch he'd cut off the D8 they kept in the local transport yard for parts.

The old caravan was a wreck that hardly kept the weather out. Jack added an awning out of permanent materials that he scavenged from around the place and when the upper Waiau River eroded enough of its bank to claim the old Boulder Reach woolshed, Jack was out in his dinghy towing bits of timber and old corrugated iron back to his terrace.

Gradually the camp grew into a permanent shack with a couple of rooms. The old caravan was relegated to storage and then was made completely redundant when a busted off limb from a beech tree caved the roof in during a storm.

Old Nor'wester Jack was happy in his shack overlooking Lake Manapouri. Ten years went by. Jack got a bit slower. But he still picked up work and scraped together a few dollars for food and beer and clothes, in that order. That's when I met him.

It was 1982 and the wife and I had just taken over the Manapouri pub. The second Tuesday after we arrived this grubby old bugger wearing a ripped Swanndri and a stockman's hat with a bit of dirty white hair sticking out from under the rim sidles into the bar and leans on the counter.

'Got any work going, mate?'

I wouldn't say it was the start of a beautiful friendship, but Nor'wester Jack was OK if you could get used to the smell. Just the bloke for cleaning out the grease traps or dealing with blockages in the plumbing. A real handy bastard to have hanging around. As long as it was in small doses.

Jack's mail used to come to the pub and we would hold it for him until he showed up to earn a few dollars. The '83 winter had been a particularly hard one and Jack's intermittent mail had begun to pile up. There was some talk around the place about sending a search party in to see if he had died but it was all a bit half-hearted and no one ended up doing anything.

At the start of October Jack bowled up to the pub as large as life to have a beer and a yarn. 'Any mail, mate?'

The bundle was passed over and Jack carefully thumbed through the envelopes. Some met with a grunt and were discarded into the roaring open fire without being read. A couple of letters with handwritten addresses were deftly folded in half and tucked into his Swanndri pocket for later.

'What's this lot?'

I cast my eye over the four remaining letters Jack had fanned across the bar. They all had the Lands and Survey belt and crown ensignia printed on the envelopes. I shrugged my shoulders.

Jack grunted, opened the first and mumbled to himself as he read the letter.

'. . . dwelling illegally on National Park land . . . remove immediately.'

Jack screwed up the letter and threw it at the fire before opening the second.

'. . . dwelling illegally on National Park land . . . remove immediately . . . final notice.'

The second letter went the way of the first and a slight smile could be seen forming in the corner of Jack's mouth as he opened the third.

'. . . remove immediately . . . consequences.'

Jack looked up a gave a laugh and opened the fourth.

'. . . Lands and Survey will demolish . . . at your expense . . .'

Jack screwed up his face, drained his handle and headed for the door.

'Better go and sort this lot out.'

It turned out that the Lands and Survey had received complaints from someone about the shack because Jack didn't have a licence to build it in the National Park. Jack had an idea about who it was but fronting up to that tree-hugger wouldn't have done any good and Jack knew it. The only way to sort it out was to go and see Ken Simons, the head of the Te Anau Lands and Survey office. Jack hitched up to Te Anau, but by the time he got there the office was closed. No worries — Jack walked around to Ken's house and banged on the front door. Ken answered.

Nobody knows what went on that night. Ken won't say and Jack just smiles. But it's not hard to guess. Ken always had a big ego on him, too big for this district — probably better suited to the city by all accounts. We all guessed that the pair of them got talking that night. Jack would've baited him, and told Ken he was a miserable bastard and such a crook shot that he couldn't even shoot his mouth off straight. Ken would have taken exception, as he fancied himself as a bit of a marksman, and the bet would have been made.

And the bet? The person who gets the most rabbits over the next couple of days wins. For Jack that meant a permit for his shack and for Ken that meant Jack would pull down his home and clear out of the park. It made for a good topic of discussion in the bar that night.

'Can I borrow your ute?' asked Jack the next day. 'I want to go out to the Wilderness.'

The Wilderness was an area of bog pine and stunted scrub that grew on poor soil out by the Mararoa River. A fair chunk of the Te Anau basin had been similar before it was brought into pasture, so this last remaining botanical oddity had been given reserve status, had stock locked out and now only ran rabbits and the odd goat.

Jack didn't want the loan of a rifle.

'Won't need one,' he muttered as he dropped the clutch on my Holden Ute and spun gravel as he left the hotel car park. I was left scratching my head. Still, it was not like Jack could shoot anyway.

Jack was back before dark with no rabbits. At this apparent lack of progress he seemed completely unconcerned.

The next day Jack was banging on the back door at nine in the morning.

'Need the ute. Come for a ride.'

I downed my coffee and followed Jack out to the garage.

News through the grapevine was that Ken Simons had picked up sixty-eight rabbits overnight and was taking the morning off work to hunt the flats around Te Anau Downs. The count-off was in the pub car park at lunchtime.

We stopped off at Henry Grant's place and hooked up his horse float. There was no one around apart from Henry's old collie barking on the end of a chain that was attached to a 44-gallon drum with the lid cut out of it.

Then we headed out to the Wilderness.

The rough gravel track that wound down through the Wilderness from the main road did no favours to the ute's exhaust pipe. After crawling the ute about two k's down the track beside the Mararoa River, Jack pulled up next to an area about a square chain in size (that's about 400 square metres in metric for you young fellas) that had been fenced with rabbit-proof wire. A sign informed all and sundry that it was a scientific research station run by the Lands and Survey to monitor the regenerative powers of the local plant life in the absence of grazing animals.

Jack got out of the ute and slammed the door.

'You ever been eeling?' asked Jack as he leant on the bonnet of the ute and rolled himself a thin cigarette.

I shook my head.

'There's two kinds of eelers in this world,' said Jack matter-of-factly. 'There's the type that goes out for a bit of fun or a feed and uses a spear, and then there's the commercial fisherman that uses nets. It's the same principle for rabbits. You can use a rifle if you want a bit of fun or a feed, or you can use a net.'

Jack walked over to the rabbit fence and stuck the toe of his boot through a hole in it before pointing his finger up the line of the fence to holes every ten yards or so. Each hole was about six inches in diameter, with seven or eight one-foot lengths of No. 8 wire poking into the reserve from the edge of each hole — just like a giant cod-pot. Rabbits go in, but can't get out.

'It's just a matter of using the right type of bait.'

The reserve had indeed illustrated the regenerative powers of the local vegetation. Inside there was plenty of young scrub regrowth and lush native grass. Outside of the reserve, by comparison, was a desert. Jack must have thrown a couple of late-season swedes in there as well to help attract the hundreds of rabbit now trapped inside the enclosure, scampering around the tangle of weeds in a mad panic at the sight of man.

Someone once said that a bird in the hand is worth two in the bush, but they can't have told Jack about it. Getting the rabbits out of the reserve and into captivity would normally have meant killing each one of them, but that must have sounded too much like hard work to old Nor'wester Jack.

Jack backed the float up to the fence, cut the netting and dropped the ramp of the float down into the reserve. Then he fashioned netting sides for the ramp from the section he'd just cut from the fence.

'We just drive them up into the float and head away,' said Jack casually as he walked around to the other side of the reserve and dropped a lit match into the thick vegetation.

The fire took a few minutes to get hold but soon the smoke and the heat and the sound of it forced all of the rabbits towards the float. There was nowhere for them to hide. The rabbits piled over each other like some sort of brown wave of ears trying to escape the flames, straight up into the float. After most of the rabbits loaded themselves, Jack simply lifted the float's ramp and bolted it shut.

'I reckon this should win that bet,' winked Jack.

We passed the volunteer fire brigade heading out to the Wilderness on our way back to Manapouri and by the time we got back to the pub the smoke was pouring into the sky and starting to form big thunderhead clouds. Someone's research project had literally gone up in smoke.

Ken was waiting in the car park, leaning on the tray of his Lands and Survey truck drinking beers from a can with three of the locals.

'Ninety-eight,' Ken shouted out as we pulled up, 'two short of the ton. Don't worry, Jack,' he grinned, 'I'm sure all the boys will chip in to get you into that retirement village down in Invercargill.'

Jack snorted and got out the car. 'Ninety-eight? You must be a bit disappointed with that tally.'

'Why, what did you get?'

'Dunno, didn't count them.'

And with that Jack dropped that ramp of the float down with a bang on the car-park gravel and hundreds of rabbits flew out everywhere.

There were rabbits heading up into the scrub, rabbits heading up into the township and rabbits flying out on the main road to be mown down by a passing stock truck. There were rabbits crashing into rabbits crashing into rabbits in a mad panic to escape. Bill Fletcher's fox terrier came screaming down from his house and was having a ball of a time going from rabbit to rabbit shaking the life out of each one before moving on to the next hapless victim. Shorty Ferson was dancing a jig around the car park: one had climbed up his trouser leg and had decided to dig its claws in. A dozen or so rabbits shot in through the open door of the pub to be met by screaming barmaids and goggle-eyed tourists. One flew under the grate of the roaring fire only to decide that it was a bit too hot before fleeing the building leaving behind it a trail of smoke and the sickly stench of burnt fur.

Ken shook his head and climbed into his truck. He knew when he'd been beaten.

There were rabbits hanging around the place for ages. Worst were the ones that had climbed up spouting or into pipes or some other inaccessible corner, got stuck, died and started to stink. The live ones stuck around too. Out of their familiar territory they sneaked around in the tussock until Bill's foxy gradually cleaned them up.

We didn't see Jack for about a month. Some of the locals reckoned he was laying low until things blew over. An official letter from the Lands and Survey arrived for Jack so I had it waiting along with a cold beer and a feed of pie when he turned up one day.

He sat down at the bar and ate.

'Good pie. What is it?' asked Jack.

I smiled at Jack. 'Well, it's been on the menu for the last month and it ain't bloody eel.'

'Nothin' wrong with it,' replied Jack with a twinkle in his eye.

A queer sort of intelligence

Stu Gibson

It was the last day of my contract: eight days of culling goats in the National Park had left me cut, bruised and totally sick of bush life. So rather than bushbash my way down to the road end, I decided to cut uphill to meet the round-the-mountain track and take the easy way out.

A quick scoot up the ridgeline and three or four creek crossings found me free of the bush and heading down and round the mountain track to the old DoC hut where I had promised myself a quick spruce-up and a drink before heading out to the road's end.

Nearing the hut a whiff of smoke drifted down the track, indicating that someone was at home and the prospect of a hot cuppa looked good.

'Gidday, mate, got a billy on by any chance?' I said as I kicked off the loose dirt from my boots at the hut door.

'It should still be hot. Just had a brew myself.'

The single occupant of the hut turned out to be

a biologist named John doing flora studies for the Department of Conservation. He was absorbed in a series of figures on one of them fancy laptop computers.

'Haven't got much use for one of them things in my line of work,' I said. 'Still, you never know with the way the world is heading these days.'

'Yeah,' John said, 'especially with the rate of development in AI.'

Fool that I am, I asked, 'What in hell's name does artificial insemination have to do with computers?'

John looked up from the screen with one of them half smiles that intelligent people save for the stupid. 'Now that's an interesting thought in future computer development.'

'Yeah,' I replied. 'George Orwell will be turning in his grave.'

John went on, 'Artificial intelligence is just a computer's way of thinking.'

'Sounds a bit like that lot down in Wellington,' I cracked.

John smiled and asked, 'Do you have a fish tank?'

'Yep,' I replied, 'but what has that to do with anything?'

'Well, if you have a fish tank, I can probably guess you are fond of animals.'

To ask a goat culler that may be seen as a little off, but I replied, 'Yep, so happens I am.'

'Right then,' says John. 'If you're fond of animals then you're probably fond of women.' Again, right on the mark.

John continued with a wry grin. 'Now if you like women you probably are partial to a bit of how's your father.' I couldn't disagree with that either.

'That's artificial intelligence for you,' he said, as his eyes returned to the screen. 'By starting with a question about a fish tank I deduced through a series of logical steps you like having sex with women.'

Well, I thought, I did ask.

My tea had gone cold by now and the subject of artificial intelligence even colder so I wished him well with his research, grabbed my kit and rifle and set off to the road end where I had arranged for my old mate Elton to pick me up.

Elton arrived eventually, but not before I'd had time for a smoke or two and run my thoughts on artificial intelligence through my head a few times just to see if I grasped the logic of it all.

'Sorry about the wait, mate, I had to bottle a batch of wine and nearly forgot about ya,' muttered Elton.

Elton had been a mate of mine for years. Odd sort of bloke really. He had lived up here by himself near the road's end for years. Ran a few beefies and sheep and generally kept himself busy studying plants and collecting antiques and, of course, making wine. You know the type — interesting, but somewhat remote.

I had been in the habit of leaving my car at his house while I was on contract and he would drop me up at the bushline and pick me up when I came out.

We talked about the usual stuff on the short drive to his house, like goat numbers, the weather and the bloke I met at the hut. I skipped mentioning the computer stuff.

'Come in and have a glass of wine before you head off,' Elton said as we pulled up in his drive.

'Nah, I think I'll just head on home for a beer and a hot bath, but thanks all the same. I'll ring you next autumn when I start my next contract,' I said. 'By the way, you don't happen to have a fish tank, do you?'

'Not bloody likely, why?' inquired Elton.

I slipped the old girl into reverse and shouted as I backed out of the drive, 'Oh no reason, see ya round sometime,' and turned onto the dusty road home.

Driving home, I recalled the last eight days: of goats killed, bluffs scaled, dunkings endured in cold streams, talk of fish tanks and dreams of soft, warm women on frost-gripped early mornings.

Yep, it will be nice to be back again next autumn, I thought. Might make a few changes next time though, like getting one of my mates in town to drop me off at the road's end. Elton was becoming much too bloody familiar for my liking!

A hell of an adventure

Trevor Hankins

It was only the second time I had been deer stalking, so needless to say I was fairly excited about the week ahead. Add to that the fact that we were planning to go to the Kaimanawa ranges, flying in then rafting down the Ngaruroro River camping along the way, finally finishing at the Kaweka ranger's headquarters.

Three of us from Auckland made the journey down to Napier to join up with 'Bloor' (short for brother in law), who was a government culler back in the days when 1080 wasn't poisoning our forests.

Kerry, who was my boss at the time, was a fairly experienced hunter having grown up in the Hawke's Bay. He was Bloor's brother-in law.

Lastly there was our mate Robbie, who also worked with us and was as green as I was, but a tough wiry little bastard who had taken pleasure in his youth by being beaten up by the infamous Sir Ge Dorr martial arts discipline.

Unfortunately for us, and even more so for the pilot, a light plane had gone missing the day before we were supposed to fly from Napier Airport into the Boyd Hut airstrip. Understandably all the pilots from the Napier Airport were out helping in the search for their colleague and our flight was postponed from 9 a.m. until further notice.

It was a beautiful day and to kill some time waiting for the call we had a few beers in the sun, checked through our gear to make sure we hadn't forgotten anything, then had a few more beers. By 12.30 it looked unlikely that we were going get our flight and we were all feeling pretty pissed off that we were going to miss out but could understand their wish to keep searching.

Bloor had a rare thought and decided to ring Taupo Airport to see if they could fly us in, which meant we would have to drive the 140 km over the hill, but at least we wouldn't lose another day. The aero club did have a couple of spare planes and would take us in if we could be at Taupo Airport by 2.30 p.m.

Panic mode! Bloor's wife kindly did the driving as by now we were fairly happy with quite a few beers consumed. The quick drive over was fairly exciting with numerous pit stops along the way, and each one was usually done with much laughter and the inevitable drive off leaving someone at the side of the road exposed to the passing tourist buses and logging trucks.

We made it to the airport about fifteen minutes late. To our relief the pilots gestured to us to start loading our gear into the little Cessnas and we joked and sniggered our way into two planes, three of us and the pilot in one, with Bloor, the pilot and the majority of our gear in the other.

What a great flight! With the effects of the day's efforts to stave off dehydration and just the buzz of knowing we were on our way we floated over the pines which melted into native bush of deep gullies and razorback ridges until we saw a handkerchief of an airstrip covered in puddles ranging in size from about the size of a bathtub to others as big as the plane we were in!

As we got nearer to our landing strip the pilot threw the plane on its ear and plummeted down at a helluva pace towards what we thought looked like an unlandable strip of water and grass! Well, we hit the runway at breakneck speed and splashed our way through the puddles with a hell of a racket swerving from side to side trying to avoid as many puddles as possible, water and mud flying in all directions. Needless to say we were all pretty quiet at this stage and I'm sure I saw a bit of a smile of satisfaction on the pilot's face having successfully scared the crap out of us.

Bloor was already on the ground having left about fifteen minutes before us and was standing at the side of the runway with all the gear and a big grin.

We thanked the pilot for an entertaining ride, to which he replied that it wasn't over yet as his takeoff would be more difficult than the landing. We watched as the little engine screamed away at top revs with the plane pitching and bucking as it splashed and aquaplaned down the strip to lift off at the last minute and bank steeply away to the left, followed eventually by the silence that we all love and one of the reasons the bush is such a magnet.

We were snapped out of the trance of watching the speck disappear towards Taupo by Bloor telling us to sort our shit out and help him carry the raft to the edge of the strip. With a bit of grunting we got the raft to the edge of the flat where it would stay the night while we made our way up to Boyd's Hut halfway up the hill for a well-earned dinner and a couple more quiet ones.

The hut wasn't one of the most friendliest I've been in, with eight others already there and a very bad-tempered black Lab that would snarl and growl at anyone who came near him.

One of the groups was cooking their dinner and

seemed to be labouring the process so we sat outside waiting and chatting excitedly about the next few days with a couple of guys from the other group. If only we had known what was in store.

About an hour and a half later the other guys were finally eating but had commandeered the fire some more by putting on their desert! At about ten we finally managed to eat and soon headed for the bunks where the other lot were already snoring. The Lab had one more go at us so Bloor told his owner to 'get that thing outside before I waste a bullet on it'. Thankfully, the bloke got the picture and tied it up away from us all. Sleep was easy then and welcomed.

We got up early to beat everyone else to the fire and took our time making our breakfast just to make a point, then, once all our gear was sorted, headed back down the hill to where the raft was, all of us glad to be leaving the most miserable bunch of hunters we had ever met!

The 150 m or so down to the river was very steep and interspersed with almost straight drops, impossible to carry anything down, so we rolled the plastic drums and raft over the edge and watched a bit nervously as they bounced towards the river all stopping inches from the edge on a small bit of flat ground amongst the rushes. We looked at each other and congratulated ourselves on what was better luck than management!

All the rifles and our dry gear was already loaded in the barrels and then strapped to the now-inflated raft, leaving one old 303 out just in case we saw a deer along the river.

Wetsuits and booties on and we were off!

Robbie was on his maiden voyage and the first set of rapids had him looking a bit nervous. When we slammed into the first rock face Robbie tried to fend off, a big no-no! He wore the end of the paddle in the ribs and spent the next couple of minutes rubbing them and groaning a lot. The remainder of the day was fairly uneventful but scary at times with one last big rapid to tumble over before we pulled into a nice flat spot beside a huge pool.

Camp was set up and we had a quick afternoon sortie to check out the surrounding area. Plenty of good fresh signs had us feeling positive and optimistic we should get on to something and fairly close to camp too, just the ticket for us city slickers more used to hunting snapper out of a boat!

With a good fire and a few beers we were about to sit down to dinner when Robbie screamed and collapsed to the ground clutching his foot. He had jumped over the fire and landed on top of the small end of the bully beef tin sharp side up, cutting through his sock and heel instantly. Bloor wanted to stitch it but Robbie wouldn't let him near it so Kerry cleaned it up and bandaged it as best he could. Not too bad, but enough to slow him down for the next day or two. To his credit, and maybe his Sir Ge Dorr training, he didn't whinge about it at all for the rest of the trip and kept up with us most of the time.

Morning came all too soon and we snuck up the gully behind our camp where we could have a good view of a couple of nice clearings which caught the morning sun on the other side of the gully. Nothing showed for a couple of hours so we made our way up the side of the gully to the top where we were in the big beech trees and kanuka with plenty of bush lawyer to keep us cautious.

After a few hours with good sign we spooked some sika deer, whistling at us and crashing off through the bush. I dropped down the side of the ridge and tried to follow a couple while the other guys carried on, not wanting too many rifles in the same area.

I caught a glimpse of a deer's rump just ahead of me but not clear enough to have a crack, but the adrenalin was pumping and I was pretty excited about it. I came to a shingle slide which dropped down to a bluff with the river about 200 m below and could see the deer's fresh tracks going across a well-used track. Without even thinking I started my way across. Halfway there I realised I had made a dumb move as I was now sliding downwards as much as I was going forward. I froze for a while and surveyed my predicament: keep going forward or back-track. I decided to back-track very carefully and deliberately. It took me twice as long to get back and my heart was pounding in my ears. Too close! I found a nice big rock which overhung the river and had a great view over the valley below. I sat there for quite some time calming myself down and getting my hands to stop shaking.

As I looked down into the river I watched a huge log of a fish cruise up the far side of the whitewater below the rapids. It would disappear into the whitewater at the head of the pool only to reappear at tail and start its feeding circuit all over again. It was an exciting sight for a fisherman and yet strangely relaxing as well. With fisherman's lies and water magnification taken out of the equation it still had to weigh close to 20 lb. I told myself one day I would be back with a fly rod!

Soon enough the boys came back down the ridge and joined me to watch this magnificent fish. Someone suggested taking a shot at it which we all agreed would be futile and just a waste of a beautiful trout.

Next day we headed up over the top and apart from plenty of sign it was pretty quiet with a couple of opportunities but never quite close enough or clear enough to bag one. We decided that night that tomorrow we would carry on down the river towards our destination.

I struggle to remember exactly how the day went but it sure was exciting.

The river is not for the faint-hearted. It's very big and very powerful. Now I know what it is like I doubt I would be so quick to go on another trip down it, or if I did I would definitely have a lifejacket and helmet on. In hindsight we were lucky we weren't hurt or worse. There are some bloody big rapids and waterfalls and I would rate it scarier than the Wairoa River, which is rated five in rafting terms. What's worse is you have no idea what's around the next corner or how big that drop is up ahead!

One such drop was not high but very sudden and narrow, forcing all the water into one small gap. As we hung on for grim death and plummeted over the drop, Robbie got spat out of the raft like he was a matchstick! When he came up for air he had lost his paddle and by the time we got him back in the raft it was long gone. Bloor hassled him, saying it was the one thing you never do no matter what happened: you don't let go of your paddle. To which Robbie replied that he should go and have sex with himself and that *he* wasn't drowning for any dumbass rule or a $40 paddle!

Well, about half an hour later all of us were flung out as we capsized after a particularly confused and nasty passage of water. We came back up to the surface and scrambled out on a bit of a beach, grabbing the raft as we went. Of course my thought was one of self-preservation and not my paddle and it too was never to be seen again. More lectures and abuse from Bloor, more back at him. It was fairly bloody frightening and bloody cold!

The rain had become steadier as the day wore on and we were starting to resemble prunes. After two trips into the winter waters, Robbie was shivering uncontrollably and his lips were starting to turn purple (he had about as much fat on him as a supermodel). I wasn't a hell of a lot better.

Bloor and Kerry knew of a hut up ahead so after about fifteen minutes we pulled up at a tributary which had a swing bridge leading up to a DoC hut where we could light a fire, warm up and have a feed.

As we crossed the swing bridge we were stopped midway by the unmistakable sound of an Iroquois chopper. It was getting closer and closer, then it appeared through the rain and mist like something out of *Apocalypse Now*. What a cool sight!

They came in really close hovering inches above the shingle bank in the middle of the river. The side door was open and we could clearly see a few soldiers inside clutching Armalites. A guy with a helmet and visor on was leaning halfway out the door having a really good look at us. Then suddenly he turned to the others in the chopper, shook his head and gave that 'wind her up' signal to the pilot. They blasted off with a clatter of rotors disappearing back into the dark misty sky.

We all just looked at each other, wondering what the hell that was all about figuring it was just some sort of exercise, but it was very exiting and very cool!

We got a fire going and had some hot soup and baked beans, slowly thawing out and feeling heaps better.

Time to go. Back into the raft not quite as excited or enthusiastic about the rest of the trip downriver as we were this morning. To make matters worse, the river was starting to swell with the rain, which had made it angrier and stronger.

One of the most amazing sights on the way down were the trout, big fat wild trout in excellent condition zipping under the raft as we slipped over their watery homes. Not just one or two trout; most pools had six to eight stunning-looking fish. Their bullet-shaped bodies responded effortlessly to a few hard beats of their tails to escape this very foreign threat to their usually quiet existence. Awesome!

Surprisingly we never saw a deer or maybe we were just too busy.

We spotted another hut about thirty feet above the river bank and pulled over to the side to check it out. It was a great hut with a tributary running down the side of it and bush towering up behind stretching way up to the ridge line and a great view over the river and up the valley opposite. There was also a helipad and we all agreed it would be a great spot to come back to via chopper some day.

Robbie and I needed paddles, so we found a couple of the old kerosene-tin lids and some nails and managed to bang them on to a couple of bits of kanuka. We were redeemed to some extent and quite proud of our little bit of Kiwi ingenuity.

The morning was getting on so we jumped back in the raft and carried on, the rain still relentless and the river starting to discolour. Half an hour later we could see up ahead that the river dropped considerably and we readied ourselves for another big rapid.

As we got closer we couldn't see any whitewater below or the rocks that usually show where the river heads and there was an unusually loud roaring sound. Oh shit! There was no rapid, just a shear drop of about fifteen feet commonly known as a waterfall!

Before we could react we were over the edge and staring straight down to the dark deep pool below. Like a car crash, the next few seconds were just a blur of water, noise and clashing of bodies and plastic barrels. As quickly as it started it was over, or so we thought, and we gathered our wits checking we were all there and making sure all the gear was still attached.

Amazingly we all ended up still in the raft up the right way and apart from a few bruises we were all OK. We started to paddle away from the face of the waterfall then realised it was sucking us back in. 'Paddle, you bastards!' one of us shouted, realising what was happening. Like a horror movie, the monster hadn't finished with us yet. Drawing us back into its den for another crack, we were slowly being sucked back in. All over to the opposite side of the raft as the pressure of the water came down on the near side pushing the raft under, it's fair to say we were all fairly worried. Just as we were sure the raft was going to flip it popped back out of the flow of water. We quickly got back on the paddles again but we were wasting our time — it pulled us back into the waterfall again and, as before, threatened to flip us. Again we were spat out and again we tried to paddle away from the rock face but it was futile.

After about three repeat performances we realised the raft wasn't going to capsize and we weren't going to be able to paddle against the incredible force of the undertow.

We discussed our predicament while every minute or so we would be hit with this giant force of water and would have to hang on tight as the raft bucked and listed precariously.

We decided Robbie and I would get over the side of the raft and push off the rock face with our feet while Kerry and Bloor would paddle frantically.

We slipped over the side while the raft was away from the face of the waterfall and got ready to push off as hard as we could. Bad move! The force of the water was incredible and threatened to force the both of us under the raft while sandwiching us between the rock face and the side of the raft! We screamed at the guys to pull us back in and were quite panicky as we could feel the water tearing at our bodies trying to force us down to the bottom of the dark pool. It took all of our effort to get back into the raft while the other two grabbed hold of our wetsuits to drag us back in over the side. Finally back in the raft and out of breath we decided that plan wasn't going to work.

After getting our breaths back we discussed it some more and Bloor decided the best move was for someone to dive over the side and swim away from the raft downstream with a rope, get down to the shallow water and pull us out. Great! Who?

We had doubts. Will anyone be strong enough to swim away? Or will they get sucked back into a watery grave? A few minutes passed with the three of us doubting his plan. He decided we couldn't sit here all day and got the rope out which was about thirty metres long, tied one end to the raft, stuck one end in his mouth and dived off the side of the raft like something out of *Rambo*! He popped up about fifteen feet away and swam strongly to the shingle beach, stood up and began to pull while we paddled.

Talk about anticlimax! It worked so well it was ridiculous to think we were stuck there for so long. Thank Christ for that! Another drama over.

A bit further down there was a DoC fly camp so we pulled over and had a bit of a walk around and a smoke, happy to have terra firma under our feet again.

That was pretty much the last of the big rapids and from here on the river had widened and had a bigger volume of water over a wider space. But it was becoming very swollen and discoloured as the rain had been fairly heavy and steady all day.

Kerry and Bloor knew their way around the Kawekas fairly well, having hunted and fished the area most of their lives, so they decided we would get down to the hut for the night and see how the river was the next day.

By late afternoon they knew we were close but were having difficulty recognising landmarks from our perspective on the river. When we turned the corner and spotted the swing bridge over the river they were pretty sure we had just gone past it. We paddled to the side of the river and all got out dragging the raft in the shallows back up the river against the flow until we found a spot to tie it up, well above the rising waters.

We sorted out what gear we wanted to take up to the hut and began the short walk back past the swing bridge and around the corner to the flat area where the hut was. Just as we spotted the hut a soldier in full camo gear stood up not fifteen feet away from us with his Armalite slung under his arm. We all got a bit of a fright as we had no idea they were there and one by one more stood up seemingly appearing out of nowhere! Some were cooking their meal and others were casually eating their dinner out of army-issue mugs. Full face camo, the lot, they looked fairly formidable and weren't much in the mood for a chat.

One approached us and casually asked where we had come from and what we were up to. He said they had watched us from the other side of the swing bridge drag our raft back up the river to which a few of them chortled to themselves, obviously amused by our antics. How they got over the bridge without us seeing them I will never know. We were obviously too busy to notice. We said goodbye, heading towards the hut and they melted back into the scrub and rushes.

When we got to the hut there was a big tower of a man with a Clutch Cargo-type jaw dressed in a green Swanndri, camo pants and suspiciously polished black boots. He was very cagey to begin with and not big on conversation, avoiding our questions of what he was doing here. After quite a long time he warmed and, realising we weren't the enemy, opened up a bit.

He was a sergeant in the SAS and it appeared we had stumbled into an SAS training exercise. Not just any excursion, but the big one for anyone wanting to get into the SAS. Get from the Taupo side of the Kaimanawas to Ohakune without getting caught as fast as you can and with no more than a sack to wear, a bit of fishing line and hook and one chicken, raw and complete with feathers, to eat between each team of four! Most choose to eat it the first day.

Every man and his dog, literally, were out to get them. At one stage an Iroquois landed and police dog-handlers jumped out. Our new friend told us the coppers love it and it gives their dogs a good workout in difficult terrain. His job was like a safety checkpoint to make sure everyone got through safely or could pull out if they were one of the many volunteer groups that did it for the challenge. None of those volunteers, I believe, had ever made it, most pulling out after about two days. The weather and toughness of the challenge had already claimed two teams, some search and rescue guys and a team from the Philippine army that had been going for about 48 hours and threw in the towel.

He told us some great stories over the course of the evening about the guys who had made it and the many who didn't. Apparently many of the guys survive by eating the raw turnips as they near Ohakune. He was one of those turnip eaters and said they taste wonderful after so long without food.

With the rain still falling we had dinner and talked some more before turning out the lantern at about midnight. The river was still rising.

What seemed like about two hours' sleep was shattered by someone pulling open the small window in the hut and shouting something very loudly. Understandably we got a hell of a fright and sat bolt upright in our bunks! The guy at the window nearly died too, probably because he expected to see one person and there were five. He shouted again, this time into the dark, something along the lines of 'Let's get the *&^%! out of here, it's a set-up!' Our sergeant friend calmly got out of his bunk, pulled on his clothes and mumbled something about he had better go and find them and for us to please stay in the hut. Sure thing! There was no way we were going outside with those crazy bastards running around.

Understandably we were now wide awake and lay there chatting to each other about what just happened.

After about twenty minutes we heard muffled voices outside and five minutes later the sarge came back in. He told us the four guys outside were part of their recruitment hopefuls and he told them not to cross the bridge and that they should go further upstream and wade it. The night had cleared a bit with just the odd big fast-moving cloud and a big moon was illuminating the night. The river, however, was still very swollen and very swift so we wondered how they would get on.

The next morning we awoke to more drizzly conditions. Outside in the rain was our pot from our macaroni cheese dinner the night before and as happens on an open fire there was a fair amount of burnt macaroni stuck to the bottom of it . . . but not any more! The pot was fairly clean and there were visible finger marks on the inside where the guys from last night had scraped out every little edible bit! Hungry? Oh yeah.

We decided we really needed to get on and finish our journey despite the very swollen river. We had no choice. We wandered down to the river and it didn't look very friendly. We headed down to where we left the raft and to our dismay it was gone! There was no way it had washed away as it was well secured and well above the river; someone had taken it along with one of our wetsuits and a pair of booties that we had left hanging in some bushes. Secretly part of me was thankful as that river looked very dangerous.

We got back up to the hut and told the sarge and he was very pissed off that it may have been one of their guys. He had a radio report at ten o'clock and would find out more then. We settled down to another day stuck in the hut playing cards. There was no way we could go for a hunt with all those soldiers with Armalites running around.

After being on the radio for some time, the sarge came back and told us that the guys the night before had decided the river was too dangerous to cross so opted for the bridge. They were predictably met on the other side by the enemy and three were captured, the fourth had run back onto the bridge and jumped off. It appears he swam to the side and found our raft — his escape. The sarge was very apologetic and said he was trying to get us flown out. Our eyes lit up, a flight in a Huey! We were all pretty excited about that and all agreed it was a much better prospect than rafting.

The day was filled in with joke-telling and cards but we were all getting a bit stir crazy. That afternoon the sarge made another radio check and had another big conversation. When he came back he told us it wouldn't be today but he was hopeful for tomorrow, which was when he was due to be airlifted out. Another night in the hut.

Our food was all but gone and we had to eat what had been left in the hut by previous hunters, trampers and fishermen. All we had left was some scroggin, chocolate and snack bars.

The sarge explained that the air force could not fly civilians without a directive from HQ, who would have to declare it as a mission and they weren't keen. But he was determined.

Early the next morning he got on the radio to find out what was happening. After about five minutes he packed his radio away and came slowly back to the hut. He didn't have to say anything; his face told us we wouldn't be flying. He was very angry at his hierarchy but there was nothing more he could do; he had pushed very hard for us.

He was to be picked up in half an hour and they would happily take our gear out but the rifles had to be broken down and we had to take the ammo. They would get it all to the rangers' HQ for us to pick up.

The chopper came in and we loaded up our gear and said goodbye to the sarge. He was a friendly, open guy with a good sense of humour and I think he enjoyed his stay with us. He apologised again and shook all our hands and disappeared into the chopper which in turn disappeared over the horizon.

We had kept one pack which we loaded up with the bare essentials — the ammo, our snack food, first-aid kit and light parka each and one rifle, forever hopeful.

The climb out from the hut was a real lung-buster but once up on the top it was fairly easy walking. We gained altitude steadily all day and sometime in the afternoon we were met with snow on the track. When we got to the top at the local trampers' hut we found enough inside for a cup of tea to have with our snacks and had a well-earned rest for an hour or so. We were all pretty stuffed but knew the worst was behind us.

We had a short climb up over the top and then it would be all downhill. What I didn't appreciate was how tough it is to walk in snow when you are already buggered. The snow was pretty deep in parts and my body wanted me to head back to the hut and lie down for the rest of the day, but we had to keep going as we were due out today and had no food worth mentioning.

Late in the afternoon as we were almost out to the road we saw a helicopter buzzing up and down the fire breaks and main track, which we assumed was just part of the exercise. We had taken a 'Bloor special' shortcut which had cut about twenty minutes off our walk but it was a long way from the main track.

The walk down the road was painfully slow and the light fading. When we finally reached the rangers' headquarters, seven and a half hours after we had left the river hut, we were told of the drama that had unfolded.

The first thing the ranger did after identifying us was to tell us to ring the police as they had been searching for us all afternoon, hence the helicopter.

We were stunned.

Bloor got off the phone after talking to the police, who said they would tell our families we were all OK but we could expect a bill for the search and rescue. He told them they could send their bill to the army as there was no way we would be paying for anything!

Apparently the sarge had got back to his base and

told his superiors that we were walking out with light clothing and no food and that if anything happened to us they would be responsible. He was very pissed off. The army decided the best thing they could do was ring the police who in turn started a rescue.

We just wanted to get home so we piled all our gear (the army had dropped it off earlier) into the car that was left for us by Bloor's wife and headed into town for a big feed of whatever we could find (but not turnips!) and quickly. The first stop was a pie at a service station and then McDonald's and KFC next. It tasted so good!

We finally got back to Kerry's mother-in-law's place, to everyone's relief. We had made the news as hunters lost in the Kawekas which really irked us and we had nothing to show for our efforts except a great story.

The soldier who took our raft was, we believe, given a commendation for his escape and using his initiative. He left the raft under a road bridge but somehow it was swept away in the flooded waters never to be seen again, along with the wetsuit. The next day Bloor received a phone call from the army saying the soldier would pay for the raft and wetsuit and true to their word that afternoon a parcel with the booties and a private cheque turned up in his letterbox for the full replacement value.

We never heard from the police again.

Kerry, myself and Robbie had a four-hour drive back to Auckland. We were all pretty stuffed but quietly satisfied with our hell of an adventure.

A drunken shepherd and a wild boar

Shaun Monk

It was lining up to be the worst hunting trip we'd ever been on. In fact it didn't look like we'd get to do any hunting at all.

A few months ago, my young mate Sparky had met a twenty-one-year-old joker after a fight in the Blue Pub of Methven. Seemed like a reasonable fella and now he'd taken up a job on a station up in North Canterbury. You could call him a farm hand or a dog walloper or a musterer but for the sake of this story we'll just call him The Shepherd.

The Shepherd knew Sparky was into a bit of pig hunting so he sent him a text message about the wild pigs he reckoned were running around everywhere on this North Canterbury station. That's right, I did say text message! It seems this technology has managed to penetrate all the way into New Zealand's back country.

Sparky was a bit short of pig dogs and a four-wheel-drive so I got the call-up: 'Monkey, pigs running around everywhere on this place up in North Canterbury. Be rude not to go for a look. Whadya reckon?' It was late January, which is a bad time of year for two reasons: firstly I was flat out harvesting grass-seed crops on the Canterbury Plains and secondly it's a bit hard on the dogs trying to hunt in the hot weather. We could only really get away for one night so decided to sneak off from work on the Friday afternoon. It wasn't going to be dark till 9.30 p.m.; we'd have plenty of time.

Friday came and things were going according to plan. We had my old Hilux loaded with an assortment of hunting gear, a few dogs and a box of beer in an otherwise bare chilly bin. We didn't take any food because The Shepherd had told Sparky on his text machine 'plenty of tucker up at the station, I'll look after ya'. We pointed the Hilux north leaving the worries of the world in a trail of diesel fumes.

Sparky's phone beeped again and it was The Shepherd asking if we could pick him up from the Hawarden pub on the way. He'd been at the annual ewe fair all day and was enjoying the after-match too much to be able to drive home . . . this is the point that it all started to go wrong.

It must have been around forty degrees and dead calm when we pulled into the country pub car park. I steered my rattly truck through a maze of flashy farm utes and managed to back the bloodstained dog box under a tree to give our dogs some shade. There were farm hands, dog wallopers, musterers, shepherds and stock agents of all sizes and states of sobriety spilling out from the bar onto the grass where they could smoke rollies. The younger ones were mostly wearing singlets, footy shorts, heavy socks and boots and a few blokes had bare feet or jandals. Some were tanned and others were just sunburnt, but they all had a hand around a big bottle of Speight's.

Sparky and I nudged our way into the crowded pub

politely greeted by everyone we passed even though we were strangers. Inside, the farm owners could easily be spotted: creamy moleskin pants, tweed jacket, checked shirt and a tie with sheep pictures. This seemed to be the standard uniform.

Eventually we found The Shepherd. He was taking centre stage in a yarn-spinning session to an audience of well-tanned fit young girls, who weren't too rough on the eye. The Shepherd's right arm was waving around as he spoke, while the left hand clutched the compulsory big bottle of Speight's. It looked to me like he was settled in for a big afternoon, so we politely ordered a few bottles ourselves and pretended not to be worried about the time slipping away.

After some time The Shepherd must have remembered the reason for us turning up in the first place and after an eternity of farewells we were finally on the road again. The Shepherd wanted to ride shotgun as he wasn't feeling too flash, reckoned he'd eaten a dodgy pie. 'You'd better slow down a bit,' he croaked, 'I get a bit carsick sometimes.' A pattern of drive-stop-spew, drive-stop-spew, repeated itself seven times before the lad finally fell asleep.

Now Sparky and I had never been to this property before but luckily I knew how to get there. We drove up a long gravel driveway to an area with sheds and stock yards and various houses scattered around amongst big macrocarpa trees, a few willows and some poplars. The Shepherd opened the Hilux door and fell out into the dust. He then picked himself up and stumbled inside to find his bed, leaving us a bit confused about what to do or where to go, now with only half an hour's daylight left to go and do it in.

We strolled into the singleman's quarters, which looked like the aftermath of a tsunami. There were booze bottles, smoke butts, dog biscuits and pie wrappers on the floor amongst well-known farming magazines such as *Country Wide*, *Straight Furrow* and *Penthouse*. The sink, bench and table were piled with dirty and broken dishes, while the windowsill struggled under a load of lighters, bottle openers, melted candles and stolen beer handles half-filled with dead flies. It bought back such fond memories of my student days.

Sparky, who is only an average-sized lad, found The Shepherd, who is a very big lad, and dragged him back outside. He wasn't too keen on doing any more travelling, but we managed to prop him up in the ute again, then I floored it up the farm track into the closest hills. Through one half-opened eye The Shepherd pointed to a gully above and muttered something about pigs. We did a U-turn, whipped back to the singleman's quarters and let the unfortunate bloke go to bed.

We quickly fitted rip collars to the three dogs, grabbed a knife belt each and started running towards a likely region with about ten minutes of light left. From a distance the gully looked good with broken patches of matagouri, manuka, tussock, green grass and swamp. We were gutted to find that the grass had actually been eaten off; there were cattle everywhere and not the slightest hint of pig sign. It was now dark and we were totally dejected so wandered back down, finding our way to the ute with torches.

The stars were out and a light breeze started to come up the valley. The chilly bin was full of cold beer so we cracked open a Speight's in an attempt to drown our sorrows, while we wondered where we should actually stay tonight and if it might just be best to make the two-hour drive back home.

The dogs obviously had other ideas; unbeknown to us they must have got wind of something and bolted off down the track. We were still sulking into our beer when we heard the unmistakable sound of dogs charging into a decent pig, having a bit of a battle and then settling in for a good loud bail.

We didn't realise that we could have driven to them, so took off into the darkness running up and down through the hilly paddocks for what ended up being over a kilometre. We arrived to find that the dogs had a large, angry wild pig bailed up in a big culvert under a gravel road. The strong smell of boar wafted out of that tunnel and you could hear the chomping of his grinders sharpening the tusks. The loud barking echoed out, making it sound like a dozen dogs were in there. At this point I was regretting leaving the rifle back in the truck, but it was so dark I would have been shooting by braille anyway.

The pig didn't like the torch peering through the steam into his tunnel and took off for the far end, leaping off a three-metre drop into a deep muddy pond followed by the dogs. We rushed over the road to see the silver-coloured boar shimmering in the moonlight as he climbed up a bank, throwing the dogs off and giving my best bitch a gouge to the chin. But the dogs did well to turn him back and into the pond again.

We were wondering how we were going to catch the feisty brute, when Sparky's young bitch charged into the pond and grabbed him by the ear. She got tossed around receiving rips under the chin, in the chest and through one layer of the rip collar protecting her throat. She wouldn't let go and her mother and sister quickly got in on the other ear and cheek, followed seconds later by me floundering in to grab his back legs and lift them out of the knee-deep water. Sparky leapt in with his knife and stuck the pig in the throat, the splashing around subsided and the battle was over. We dragged the fat heavy boar out of the muddy pond and up onto the track before gutting him. After praising the dogs for their good work we wandered back up the track to the Hilux and finished our still-cold beers. We arrived back to the singleman's quarters at about 11.30 p.m. and hung the boar in a handy shed.

I awoke to the sound of The Shepherd rattling pots and pans in the kitchen at 4 a.m. He was as chirpy as a fantail and cooking up a feed of bacon and eggs, so we presumed it was breakfast time. He promised he'd look after us for tucker and he did. We slurped down some strong coffee while we ate. 'Righto, fellers, time to go hunting,' the Shepherd decided.

'Sounds good, mate,' replied Sparky, 'but you'd better come and have a look at the boar we caught about six hours ago.'

We didn't think there was much need to fill him in

on the minor details of our evening hunt. He redeemed himself well with a great tour around the property and the dogs even managed to catch another couple of pigs.

All too soon we were heading back towards the Canterbury Plains. A familiar beep screeched out of Sparky's phone. 'Hey Monkey,' he said after reading for a minute, 'this bloke I know down Waimate way reckons there's pigs running around everywhere on his old man's farm. Wants us to come down for a look next weekend. Be rude not to. Whadya reckon?'

Kiwis abroad

Who says New York's big?

Dianne Haworth

Two Kiwis living in London, Blackie and Rabbit, had bought their tickets to join their mates on a cheap weekend trip to New York; however, a heavy night in the local pub prior to their early-morning departure saw them miss the flight. To add to their woes Blackie, in the course of that evening, had also accidentally wiped out his friends' text contacts on his mobile and couldn't remember which hotel they were booked into.

What to do? The pair decided to go anyway and turned up at Heathrow Airport some time the next day, Blackie's logic being, 'Look, New York can't be that bloody big. We'll find them.' Meanwhile, their friends Kate and Andy, who hadn't heard from them and didn't have the mobile connections for New York/London, decided to get on with it and explore the Big Apple.

'Take us to the Empire State Building,' Blackie told the cab driver at JFK airport. It was the only place whose name he could think of, and after being dropped off with their baggage in front of the iconic building, Rabbit glanced down the street. 'Blackie! For God's sakes, there they are!' he shouted as Kate and Andy swung into view.

'Told ya,' Blackie said.

Humpty dummies

Paul Staunton

While I was travelling around Australia with a mate we stumbled across a pub in Humpty Doo in the Northern Territory. With the locals just being their bizarre selves, we decided to sit for a while.

We got talking and drinking cold ales from the tap after a great but stinking hot day, when the locals told us that the fishing club was having a do on that night.

We stayed, but at the end of the night had to drive two kilometres to a camping spot for the night. There was a policeman outside the pub waiting for the first person to take off for home as everyone in the pub was drunk (and driving).

One person in the pub was not drinking so I suggested that he walk outside, pretend to stumble to his car, and drive off very quickly in the opposite direction to which most of us were going.

He took off in his car. The policeman gave chase and everybody piled out into their cars and straight home. Everyone got home alive, well, and without coming across the constabulary.

One of the funniest sights was watching all the people run for their cars as if there was a breakout at the prison.

We called back the next day and they were still laughing; I think they were still drunk too.

Blind drunk

Mark Dennis

On a trip to Europe back in 1983 we were staying in a caravan park near Hamburg. After getting settled we went to visit the nearby bottle shop and after much deliberation we decided to buy two cartons of 500 ml stubbies of beer.

There were four of us and we were attracted by the novelty value of a half-litre stubby and the fact that it was the cheapest beer in the shop.

A party awaited!

We got back to the caravan park later that afternoon and started drinking and did not stop until the wee hours of the morning when almost all the beer was gone. The beer had contributed to a good night and we all slept like logs.

On waking the next day, all feeling a little seedy and sheepish, we'd started to clean up the empty bottles when the caretaker approached. We thought we might be in trouble for drinking all night, but the bloke just cleared his throat and said in broken English, 'Well done, you've probably just broken some sort of beer-drinking record. I've never seen anybody drink so much non-alcoholic beer.'

To say there were four red-faced travellers was an understatement.

Collecting glasses

Kevin Bradley

My favourite yarn happened while my wife and I were touring Europe. We'd been travelling all over the continent enjoying foreign beers and, of course, collecting the usually quite decorative glass (as you do).

Whilst in Rome we went to a quaint little café and bar to enjoy a Peroni Nastro Azzurro or three. The glass looked quite collectable and it had my name written all over it. So I told my wife to whack this glass into her handbag, then we quickly left.

Anyway, we'd gone fifty metres down the road when the waiter came running after us, shouting something in Italian.

We looked at each other and thought, 'Should we run or face the consequences? I mean, what could they do? It's only a glass.' So we stood our ground.

The waiter came scurrying towards us talking very quickly in Italian. We were very worried.

Then from behind his back he pulled out our camera which we'd left behind in the rush.

We thanked him in the only Italian we knew — a tip.

We both heaved a big sigh of relief — but my wife gave me a serve over leaving the $400 camera for a $2 glass.

Snake bite

Bert and Bill were great old mates and they loved nothing better than a spot of fishing. They had planned an overseas trip to a remote part of outback Australia where they had heard the codfish were monsters.

On the second day of their holiday, disaster struck. Bill had responded to the call of nature and while squatting behind a tree, he was bitten on the dick by a black snake. Bill went into a panic as the snake slithered away, revealing its distinctive red belly.

'Bert! Bert! You've got to do something quick. Fetch a doctor!'

Bert knew he had to move fast so he went to get the Flying Doctor Service. Off he raced to the cattle station they had passed earlier, and asked to use the telephone. He spoke with the in-service doctor, who explained that Bert would have to follow his instructions if he was to save his mate's life.

'OK, OK, tell me what I have to do,' he pleaded.

The doctor told Bert that he must make a cut across the bite with a sharp knife and then suck the poison out of the wound.

Bert raced back to the campsite, where he found Bill in a desperate mood.

'What did the Flying Doctor say?' Bill screamed with obvious terror.

Bert looked at him, shook his head slowly, and said: 'Bill, he said you're going to die.'

The last word

Feeling down

Martin Crump

A couple of weeks ago my wife wasn't feeling too good about herself — she was moping about the house with a face like a half-chewed Throatie.

It's terrible to see yer loved one like this. She was wandering around the house — we have two full-length mirrors in our bedroom and do you know what she did? She stripped off naked in front of these mirrors and sat on the edge of the bed just looking at her reflection in the glass. Just then I walked in and she turned to me and said, 'I'm feeling fat and ugly, Marty, pay me a compliment would you?'

Well, I looked at her for a bit and I said, 'You know, Jill, one thing about you is . . . you've got fantastic eyesight.'

Did you hear the one about . . .

Did you hear the one about the Great Dane, the German shepherd and the poodle?

The three of them were sitting at the vet's waiting for their turn and they got to talking, as you do. The German shepherd said to the poodle, 'What are you here for?' 'Oh,' he said, 'Well, the postie rides past the house every morning with those bloody wheels going round and I couldn't stand it any more so I jumped at him and tore at his legs, scratching and biting. I tore them to shreds, so I'm for it — they're putting me down today.'

'Geez, back luck,' said the Great Dane.

'What are you in for?' the poodle asked the German shepherd. 'Oh,' said the shepherd. 'We live next door to a family with young kids. They are as noisy as hell and they consider it great sport to annoy the dog over the fence, and that's me. Let me tell you, I was patient. I put up with sticks poked in my face and ears. I put up with them jumping on my back, kicking and screaming until I couldn't stand it any more. I snarled, turned on two of them and had a little fun of my own. I did put a few nasty gashes on them, so I'm for it; they are putting me down today.'

'Geez, too bad,' said the Dane.

So the poodle asked the Great Dane why he was at the vet's. 'Well,' said the Dane, 'I was at home lying on the couch watching Sky Sports when the lady of the house came in and started to do the housework. She was waggling around the couch wearing this slinky little number and it got so I couldn't stand it any long so I crept up behind and gave her a real good seeing to; I rode her like there was no tomorrow!'

'Oh,' said the poodle and the shepherd, 'you're for it; they will be putting you down today as well!'

'No, actually,' said the Dane, 'I'm just in to have my claws trimmed.'

Something special

Jack Stafford

An old, white-haired man walked into a jewellery store in Christchurch one Friday evening with a beautiful young girl at his side. He told the jeweller he was looking for a special ring for his girlfriend.

The jeweller looked through his stock and brought out a $5000 ring. The old man said, 'No, I'd like to see something more special.'

The jeweller went to his special stock and brought another ring over. 'Here's a stunning ring at only $40,000,' the jeweller said.

The young lady's eyes sparkled and her whole body trembled with excitement.

Seeing this, the old man said, 'We'll take it.'

The jeweller asked how payment would be made and the old man replied, 'By cheque. I know you need to make sure my cheque is good, so I'll write it now and you can call the bank Monday to verify the funds and I'll pick the ring up Monday afternoon,' he said.

Monday morning, the jeweller phoned the old man. 'There's no money in that account.'

'I know,' said the old man, 'but let me tell you about my weekend!'

Meet your match

Martin Crump

When it comes to meeting the ladies, the gift of the gab is a handy tool to have and Phil had it in spades.

He was the epitome of smooth. One night we were all at a dance and I witnessed this in action. We were helping to clean up at the end of the night, when Phil, with an armload of gear, spun around, and knocked this very attractive lady right in the bosom.

Quick as a flash he said how sorry he was, adding, 'I know if your heart is as soft as what I've just hit, then you will forgive me.'

And she replied, 'I know that if the rest of you is as hard as your elbow, then I'll meet you in the car park after the dance!'

They are still dating, I believe.

Hoodwinked

Jeanie Molloy

A friendly local butcher, who knew everyone in the district, was very puzzled one day when a girl came in holding a baby. He asked her, 'Where did you get that from?'

She replied, 'Don't you remember? Nine months ago you had the day off.'

For once he was dumbfounded. The woman continued, 'So, what are you going to do about it?'

He scratched his head for a while, very embarrassed and said, 'I'll tell you what I'll do. I'll give you free meat until the boy is thirteen.' So away she went.

The years rolled by and the boy (being a regular customer) was getting bigger and bigger, so one day the butcher says, 'And how old are you now, sonny?'

The boy replied, 'I will be thirteen tomorrow.'

Rubbing his hands with glee, the butcher said, 'You go home and tell your mother that after tomorrow there will be no more meat and watch her face.'

So away the boy goes and tells his mother. Her response? 'Well, you go back and tell him I've been getting free meat, free bread and free groceries for the last thirteen years and watch his face.'

Old men can think quick!

Jack Stafford

An elderly farmer in Marlborough had owned a large property for several years. He had a dam in one of the lower paddocks where he'd planted some fruit trees, plums, apricots and nectarines. The dam had been fixed up for swimming when it was built and he also had some picnic tables placed there in the shade of the fruit trees.

One evening the old farmer decided to go down to the dam to look it over, as he hadn't been there for a while. He grabbed a ten-litre bucket to bring back some fruit. As he neared the dam, he heard voices shouting and laughing with glee. As he came closer he saw it was a bunch of young women skinny-dipping in his dam.

He made the women aware of his presence and when they saw him they all went to the deep end.

One of the women shouted to him, 'We're not coming out until you leave!'

The old man frowned. 'I didn't come down here to watch you ladies swim and I'm certainly not interested in seeing you get out of the dam naked.' Holding the bucket up he said, 'I'm here to feed the eels.'

Moral: Old men may walk slow, but they can still think fast.

Pipe wisdom

Bert never took his treasured pipe out of his mouth. When he travelled up to Auckland, he was forced to share a rail carriage with a cranky old woman who objected to the pipe from the moment he sat down.

'I'll have you know that my husband is nearly seventy and never once has he put a pipe in his mouth.'

Bert thought about this as he gently sucked at the tobacco.

'That so, missus? I should tell you that I'm nearly eighty and I've never put it anywhere else.'

A new suit could make you feel better

Scots Kiwi

There was this man who had been putting up with this terrible pain in the groin area for months, so he decided to see his doctor about it. He explained to his doctor how this pain started in his groin area and travelled from there to the appendix area and from there on to his navel. The doctor asked some questions, then went on and examined his tummy, pressed and probed, asked some more questions, stood back and said to the man that his medical problem was quite serious and that it was his opinion that he would have to have an operation to have his testicles removed to obtain a cure. He told the man to go home and think seriously about it.

The man had been putting up with so much pain that after a few weeks went back to his doctor and asked the doctor to go ahead and arrange the operation since he still was in shocking pain. The operation was a complete success, all the pain had gone, but the man was still feeling a bit depressed and out of sorts, so he decided to have a new suit made to measure by a tailor, thinking that it might make him feel much better.

The tailor measured him for the jacket, then onto his trousers, taking his waist measurement first, then onto his outside leg, then inside leg. He then asked the man, 'What side do you hang your private parts?'

The man laughed and said, 'Don't worry about it, it makes no difference.'

'No difference!' screamed the tailor. 'Don't you know that if your trousers are cut wrong, you can get an unbearable pain that starts in the groin area, then travels to the appendix area and then up towards your navel?'

Poetry prizes
Jack Stafford

A group of those pompous people who love poetry that often doesn't rhyme, and can't be understood by the sane, were having a meeting. They had decided upon the Fox Glacier hotel for this occasion and were making the most of it.

They were joined by an old goldminer who explained that he was interested in poetry and just wanted to listen.

Towards the end of the meeting they had a competition for an 'off the cuff' poem where the final word had to be Timbuktu. The prize was a book of poems written by the organiser and the winning poem was:

Out into the desert sand
Looking for the promised land
Go the camels two by two
Destination Timbuktu.

The old fellow stood up and said that he wanted to have a shot at the competition. They tried to explain that it was over but he couldn't be silenced.

Finally for the sake of peace they relented. The old goldminer stood. And spoke:

Me and Tim a tramping went
Met three girls in a pop-up tent
They was three and we was two
I bucked one and Tim bucked two.

They had to give him the prize.

The fox hat

Prince Charles, the Prince of Whales and Dolphins, was to officially open the Eketahuna Heritage Centre and there was lots of interest from the international press. When the time for the grand opening arrived, he came out on stage wearing a ridiculous-looking fox-fur hat — totally inappropriate for the New Zealand countryside! Everyone attempted to be polite and not ask him about the hat until, at the civic reception, the local newspaper journalist couldn't hold back.

'Sir, I have one question and it is about your hat. Why are you wearing a fox-fur hat?'

Prince Charles looked sympathetically at the man and replied: 'I'm pleased you asked me that question because it has also puzzled me. Mummy told me to wear it. I was up very early to get the plane from Heathrow and as I left the castle, I knocked on Mummy's chamber door and told her I was off to New Zealand to open the Eketahuna Heritage Centre, and I'm positive that she said: "Wear the fox hat!"'

Christmas
Hazel MacKrell

The minister of a local church asked his congregation if next week they could bring a little something along to church that represented Christmas. Some brought decorations for the tree. Some brought presents, others brought food for those that would be by themselves, but one elderly gentleman shuffled up to the altar and placed a pair of ladies' knickers down. The minister looked at him and asked in a very shaky voice, 'Carol's?'

Golden anniversary

Well, there was this old couple who had been married for fifty years. They were sitting at the breakfast table that morning when the old gentleman said to his wife, 'Just think, honey, we've been married for fifty years!'

'Yeah,' she replied, 'just think, fifty years ago today we were sitting here at this breakfast table together.'

'I know,' said the old man. 'We were probably sitting here naked as jaybirds fifty years ago.'

'Well,' Granny snickered, 'what do you say? Should we?' The two stripped to the buff and sat down at the table. 'You know, honey,' the little old lady breathlessly said, 'my nipples are as hot for you as they were fifty years ago.'

'I wouldn't be surprised!' replied Gramps. 'One's in your coffee and the other's in your oatmeal!'

Caught in the bluff
Jack Stafford

Two old drovers were standing at the bar yarning away when one said, 'I remember a time when I drove a flock of a thousand ewes from Gisborne to Wairoa.'

The second old guy said, 'I drove two thousand ewes from Gisborne to the Waikato.'

After a minute, the first guy said, 'I drove three thousand ewes from Gisborne to Levin.'

There was a silence then the other guy replied, 'I drove five thousand ewes from Gisborne to Blenheim.'

'How did you get over Cook Strait?' said the first guy.

There was a long silence then the second guy replied, 'We didn't go that way.'

The American hunters
David McClelland

Two overseas hunters turned up one day looking for good hunting territory. They drove up to the local pub in their jeep and in their deep American drawl said, 'What sort of wildlife would we be able to shoot up the back of the station, boy?'

Well, the local a little under the weather replies.

'Well, mate, let me see, there's wild pigs, oh and wild deer and of course sheep.'

'Wild sheep?' the American said in amazement. 'We have never heard of wild sheep.'

'They will be, mate, when you start chasing and shooting them.'

Street smarts

Jack Stafford

He was a tractor driver, a bulldozer pusher. In the US of A they'd call him a Cat skinner. Something to do with the old-time mule skinners. He was in this pretty flash restaurant and he was with his lady love, she was a little beaut. Everybody who came in took a second look at her. He himself was a pretty noticeable fellow with a nose which had survived a good few collisions and the build of a competition chopper. He noticed a couple of guys come in and sit down not too far away. They kept casting serious glances towards his table and he knew they were not admiring him.

He recognised the guys as a couple of the bosses from the company he worked for. One was a civil engineer and the other a jerk from admin.

They called the waiter over and one started scribbling something on a piece of paper. The waiter brought the paper over and placed it in front of the driver. He looked up at the men and both of them looked away. Slowly and without moving he read the message:

The engineer thinks that he was with you at Canterbury University and I went through Victoria with a student you remind me of. We would like to join you for a drink and a yarn. Nod when you're ready and we'll come on over. It's all on us.

Smiling, the driver picked up the pen, turned the paper over and wrote:

I am a bulldozer driver. I never went to any university but I did a course with the International School of Taxidermy and I became an expert with birds. I'm looking after this pigeon myself. Stay where you are if you know what's good for you.

Tragedy at the brewery

You heard about the brewery worker who fell into the vat of beer and drowned?

At the inquest the coroner thanked the man's colleagues for doing their best to save him and told the family it was a terrible tragedy but at least their relative died a quick death.

'Be buggered,' yelled one of his mates. 'It was a very slow death. He got out to piss three times.'

Animal antics
Jack Stafford

There was this primary school in one of the rural areas near to Matamata. The sweet young school-mistress had started her class and the pupils had settled down when in stepped another pupil, late and a little flustered by not arriving on time.

'You're late, Frank,' the teacher said to the boy. 'What has held you up?'

'I had to take some heifers down to the bull,' answered the boy.

'I thought your father could have done that?' said the teacher.

'No,' answered Frank. 'It has to be a bull.'

When a stutter can mean so much

Scots Kiwi

A married man had a very bad stutter and his wife found it an embarrassment when with him in company and was forever asking him to see his doctor as she thought something could be done to help improve his speech. So the husband went and saw his doctor. After a couple of visits the doctor told him there was a cure, but it involved an operation to remove five centimetres from his penis. The doctor told him to go home and discuss it with his wife.

A few more months passed and, as always when they were in company, his wife as usual got embarrassed. The husband and wife spoke again about his stutter, and they decided that he should go and get the operation done. The operation was a complete success. Within weeks the husband, who was very intelligent, was touring the country giving lectures on various subjects. Meanwhile the wife was missing the good sex life they had been having before the operation and it was getting her down, so she told her husband that she would be happy if he could get the operation reversed, so the husband went back to his doctor and asked him to reverse the operation.

The doctor sat in his chair for a minute before speaking with a stutter, 'Tt th th there iii is n n n no wa wa way t t t the op op op oper oper operation cc co co could b b b be re re re rever rever reversed.'

Times were tough
Megan Simmonds

Grandad was not known for his generosity. One night the roast of beef was a bit small, so he offered the children a penny if they went without meat. There were plenty of takers.

Grandma uncapped the steam pudding, brought out the golden custard and cream. 'OK,' said Grandad, 'who'll pay a penny for a serving of pudding?'

Life savers
Jack Stafford

A middle-aged woman was driving around Lake Rotoiti. Taking a corner too fast she got into a slide and with a crash her car went through a fence, down a small cliff and sank into the lake.

Two young boys were cycling behind and witnessing the accident, dropped their bikes then jumped into the lake. With great difficulty they managed to get hold of the woman and drag her from the car. They got her up the beach and working hard they managed to get her breathing again.

Finally she got her breath back and sat up. 'You boys have saved my life. What can I do for you?'

'No problem,' said one. 'Just so long as you're OK.'

'No, no,' said the woman, 'I'm the Prime Minister of New Zealand. I can give you anything. Let me buy you a new mountain bike with all the trimmings. One for each of you.'

One boy smiled but the other had a very worried look.

'Why do you look so worried?' she said to this boy.

'My dad used to be a fighter pilot at Ohakea,' he replied. 'When he finds out whose life I've saved he's going to kill me.'

WYBMADIITY

A bloke walks into a country pub and sees a sign with the letters WYBMADIITY above the bar. Confused and intrigued, he asks the barman what the letters stand for.

Barman replies: 'Will you buy me a drink if I tell you?'

Bloke says: 'Sure, but what do the letters stand for?'

Barman again replies: 'Will you buy me a drink if I tell you?'

Bloke says: 'I said that I would, so what is it?'

Barman replies: 'Will you buy me a drink if I tell you?'

Bloke says: 'Yeah, yeah, just tell me what the letters stand for.'

Barman replies: 'Will you buy me a drink if I tell you?'

Bloke says: 'You're a bloody broken record with bad hearing. What is it?'

Barman replies: 'Will you buy me a drink if I tell you?'

Bloke says: 'I give up.'

And then the barman came clean and explained to the bloke what WYBMADIITY means . . . again.

New Zealand hospitality

Scots Kiwi

Here I was just arrived in Palmerston North, flown in from Australia, a young Scotsman sent here on a work's contract. New Year's Eve, alone in a strange city, knowing no one, I called a taxi from the city square about 8.45 p.m. to go home for a lonely quiet evening, armed with a half-bottle of whisky and a few beers.

The taxi pulled up for me and as I got in my door, the other door on the roadside got opened by a young lady who had crossed from the shops. The driver told her the taxi was mine, but I interjected by saying if we were going in the same direction we could share the taxi and that would be OK.

We started talking and I said I had just arrived in New Zealand and knew no one, so she invited me to her place. When we got there she put on some records. I sorted out a few drinks, we had a few dances, she made me a meal, we had a few more drinks, then a few kisses and a few cuddles, she then asked me to stay the night. What a great night it turned out to be.

In the morning when I awoke I could smell the bacon and eggs cooking. When I got up she told me to have a shower, then sat me down to a good breakfast. We chatted for a bit, I phoned for a taxi and when I was ready to go out the door she asked me if I had had a good time. I said yes, a great time. She then said, how about some money, Jock. I said to her that she had been so nice and so good to me that I could not take money from her as well.

One night at the pub

These three blokes have been out working on a building site all day when they decide to go for a beer. Unfortunately the local has been yuppified and the bouncer tells them they can't come in because they aren't wearing ties. One of them pulls off his sock, ties it around his neck and fronts the bouncer again who lets him in. The other grabs the belt from his trousers, ties it around his neck and he's let in.

The last bloke hasn't got socks or a belt so he runs back to the car and grabs the jumper leads and ties them around his neck.

The bouncer looks at him and says, 'You can come in, but don't go starting anything!'

Man's best friend

A couple of blokes were lost up in the snowfields and sure they were about to die. All of a sudden a kelpie came bounding over the pass with a small keg of beer around his neck, in much the same fashion as the famous St Bernards of the European Alps.

'Look at that,' said one of the blokes. 'Man's best friend has come to our rescue.'

'Yeah,' said the other. 'I think the dog wants to help too.'

Off his rocker

This bloke's been at the pub all night and is totally tanked when the barman tells him to go home and sleep it off. After a bit of an argument and a little sulking the guy says, 'Well, bugger you then, I'll take my custom somewhere else!'

He gets off the stool and falls flat on his face. People rush to help him up but he tells them to 'bugger off' and tries to do it himself.

'God, I'm more pissed than I thought,' he thinks and giving up on the idea of standing he drags himself across the floor and to the door where he falls down the few steps to the footpath.

'I'll just lie here and get some fresh air,' he thinks, but even that doesn't work because every time he drags himself upright he falls down again.

Fortunately he only lives a few houses up the street so he just drags himself along until he gets to his front door.

Reaching up for the door knob he drags himself up so he can get the key in the lock and again falls down on his face.

Giving up on walking he drags himself down the hall, up onto the bed and next to his wife who mutters in her sleep about smelling like a brewery, being out all night, the dinner going cold and all that trivial stuff.

Before she can get a head of steam up the guy is asleep and so is she.

The next morning the missus wakes him early and starts again.

'You must've really had a big one last night,' she says.

'What makes you say that?' says the bloke whose head is hosting a private show by AC/DC.

'Well, the pub rang this morning and said you'd left your wheelchair behind again,' she says.

Stringing it out

Have you heard the one about the three pieces of string who decide they want to experience the good life inside a pub?

The first two slick themselves down, straighten themselves up and walk up to the bar and ask for a beer.

'Sorry,' says the barman. 'We don't serve string around here.'

The third has hung back, and hearing that he figures he might try a different approach. He twists himself round into a knot and frays his ends before walking to the bar.

The barman is not impressed.

'Hey, I told your friends we don't serve string here; you are a piece of string, aren't you?' he says.

'Nah, I'm a frayed knot,' comes the reply.

Never felt better

Farmer Mike O'Hearn appeared in court charged over his negligence in allowing his stock to stray all over the main road. A passing semitrailer had run right into the herd, killing several beasts and causing severe bodily injury to O'Hearn, his horse and his dog. Under cross-examination by the prosecutor, the drover confirmed that his first words to the attending police officer were: 'I've never felt better in my life.'

When asked to explain this strange comment, the drover said: 'Well, there I was, spread-eagled on the road, with a busted arm and leg and surrounded by this carnage. The police officer came up to my horse, which was bleeding from both nostrils and in great distress, put his pistol to its head and pulled the trigger. Then he went over to my dog, which was in an awful mess, and did the same. Then he walked over to me and said: "How are you, O'Hearn?" I took a look at his pistol and quickly responded: "I've never felt better in my life."'

De-ducks

The farmer had a look that would have soured milk when asked how his crops had turned out.

'De-ducks got the bloody crop.'

'Ducks!' the inquirer exclaimed in surprise.

'No,' was the reply, 'not ducks — de-ducks. I shipped a good number of truckloads of wheat all right, but the bastards de-ducks the road freight, they de-ducks the insurance, they de-ducks the handling charges, and when they gets through, I'm buggered if the de-ducks haven't got all of me money.'

He knows when he's had enough

Two shearers were getting stuck into the grog. Suddenly, one of them tumbled off his bar stool and rolled across the floor and lay there without moving a muscle or a hair on his head.

'One thing about Bill,' his drinking mate offered to the worried barman, 'he knows when to stop.'

Satan!

Mrs O'Toole had about enough of her husband's drinking sprees and decided to try and scare him out of his habit. One Friday night, she hid herself behind a thick bush and waited for him to roll his way home from the pub. When he came along the track she jumped out in front of him.

'Struth! Who the hell are you?' he cried.

'Satan!' came the deep, disguised reply.

Bill O'Toole's hand shot out like an arrow. 'Shake hands, you old son of a gun! I married yer sister!'

Dead-end drinkers

Two old-timers had been drinking at the same hotel bar on the same day, at the same hour, every week for nigh on fifteen years. One day, only one of the men arrived.

'Where's your mate?' asked the barman with obvious surprise.

'He got burned,' replied the old fellow with a forlorn shake of his noggin.

'Cheer up,' said the barman, 'he'll be up and around again soon.'

'Don't know about that,' answered the lonely one, glumly. 'I don't think they mess about down at that there crematorium.'

Worldly thoughts

Bill had reached the age of fifty and had never owned a suit. He'd even gotten married in a rented tuxedo. His 30th wedding anniversary was approaching, so he decided to get the best tailor in New Zealand to make him a suit for the celebration.

The tailor showed him an enormous range of cloth and after he had selected a nice length of grey wool, the tailor started to measure him up for the suit. Bill chatted away, saying how pleased he was to have the best tailor in the country making his first suit and how proud he would be in four weeks when he arrived at the anniversary party.

The tailor looked up and snapped: 'That settles it! I cannot make your suit.'

Bill stared back in amazement. 'But that's ridiculous,' complained Bill. 'I've selected the cloth, you've measured me and you're the best tailor in New Zealand.'

The tailor looked at Bill and explained. 'It is because I am the best tailor in the country that I cannot make your suit — I simply cannot make a suit in four weeks.'

'But,' spluttered Bill, 'the good Lord made the world in seven days, yet it takes you more than four weeks to make a suit?'

'Yes,' replied the tailor, 'but have you had a good look at the world lately?'

A big future

The young farm boy left school without learning to read and write and found himself down in the nearest town looking for work. After a week it became obvious that without these vital skills, he didn't have a lot of choice when it came to jobs, so he reluctantly applied for a position as a toilet attendant at the local factory. His duties were to wash down the toilets and keep a weekly record of all the cleaning products he used. After explaining that he couldn't write, the foreman told him he wasn't suitable for the job.

Dejected and rejected, he roamed the streets and finally sat down on an old wooden fruit case. As he pondered his frustrating situation, he became angry and kicked the fruit case to pieces. As he surveyed the damage, an idea struck him — to collect the pieces of wood and sell them as firewood. He made a few cents and decided to buy a few old crates from the local fruit shop. He chopped these up and sold them for firewood and made a few dollars. He continued buying and selling until he had enough money to go to the timberyard and buy some decent wood. Eventually, he had enough money to buy the timberyard.

As the years passed, he was able to buy the local forest and then he purchased timber holdings all over New Zealand. He had become a multimillionaire. The time had come for him to expand internationally, and while negotiating with America's largest mill operation, the company's head honcho insisted on a written agreement to seal the deal.

'Can't do that,' the Kiwi said. 'Never did learn to read or write.'

The American was dumbfounded. 'But you're the most successful timber merchant in New Zealand and a multimillionaire! For God's sake, man, what would you have aspired to be if you had been able to read and write?'

The Kiwi looked long and hard at the American and replied: 'A toilet attendant.'

Moth balls

An American tourist was visiting the a small town and staying in a country pub. One day the hotel maid was cleaning his room when she opened the cupboard and a moth ball rolled out. This puzzled the Yank, who stared at the round white ball on the carpet.

'Say, missy, what is that white thing that rolled out of the cupboard?'

'That, sir,' replied the maid, 'is a moth ball.'

'Gee whiz,' said the surprised American tourist, 'some moth!'

Old Bill in the big smoke

Old Bill was making his first trip to the big city and found himself in Smith & Caughey's. He was dazzled and he walked from floor to floor until he found himself in the women's clothing department. He stood there, totally mystified, staring as an elderly woman stepped into the changing rooms. A security guard approached him and asked him if anything was wrong, but Old Bill just gazed in amazement as a young girl emerged from the same changing rooms.

'I'll be darned!' was all Old Bill could manage to say. 'I knew I should have brought the old lady with me.'

You wouldn't believe it!

Five blokes decided to go fishing, out past the heads where they had been told they could catch 'the big 'uns'. The captain of the boat had given them a list of instructions, starting with the all-important fact that they should definitely have a solid breakfast — even if the boat was leaving at 3.30 a.m. Now that was all very well for a seasoned sailor to say, but you should try eating at some ungodly hour of the morning when your eyes insist on closing.

Off they sailed and about an hour later, they hit the swells and the fishing was terrific. An hour after that, there were even bigger swells. One of the blokes had obviously not eaten breakfast — he had broken the number-one rule! There was all manner of retching and groaning as he threw up into the sea. Next thing, he turned to his mates and explained that as he had thrown up, his false teeth had accidentally tumbled into the briny. He looked a little like a gummy shark, and his mates couldn't help but laugh. This made the man even more miserable.

One of the men decided to play a prank on his friend, so he took out his own dentures and hooked them up to his fishing line and gently lowered them into the sea. Five minutes later, he shouted out that he had got a 'bite' and proceeded to wind up the line in full view of the sick feller.

'Whoa, what have I got here? Cor blimey, you wouldn't read about it! I think I've hooked your teeth!'

The sick one looked up, incredulous, and the colour was already coming back into his cheeks as he snatched the teeth and tried to place them in his mouth. All of a sudden, he chucks them overboard and comments: 'Wouldn't you know my luck — they're some other bastard's!'

I'll buy that

The city slicker was determined to buy a horse at the monthly stock auction and waited patiently as each horse was offered and sold. Halfway through the auction, they led in an old and obviously clapped-out beast that looked like it should have been headed for the knackery. The city bloke started bidding enthusiastically until the surprised auctioneer slammed the hammer down.

'Sold!' he announced.

The farmer seated next to the city slicker couldn't help himself, and leant over to the man and politely asked: 'What do you plan to do with him?'

The city slicker, looking as pleased as Punch, announced: 'Race him!'

The farmer looked at the old horse and then back at the city slicker.

'Yes, you should win!'

A quick one

Bill the shearer's cook was well known as a cadger, so when he bailed up Smithy the local off-duty copper, he tried his best to strike up a conversation.

'What about a quick one?' asked Bill.

'Don't drink,' replied Smithy.

'Have a cigarette then?'

'No, thanks, don't smoke.'

'Ever had any headaches?' inquired Bill.

'Yes, pretty often these days,' replied Smithy.

'Just as I thought! Your halo's too bloody tight!'

Road directions

Completely lost on a country road somewhere in the wops, a tourist slammed on the brakes and pulled his car over to stop beside a farmhand who was trudging along in the scorching midday sun.

'I say,' called the driver, 'can you give me the directions to the next town?'

'Yeah,' replied the farmhand, as he wiped a flow of grimy sweat from his brow. 'You turn right at the next crossroad, travel about ten miles until you spot a big shed, turn right again until you see a big pine tree, then turn right again until you come to a train line, then turn right.'

An hour later, the same car came bouncing down the same road and the car once again pulled over to where the farmhand was seated, resting under a pine tree.

'I never could follow directions,' said the tourist. 'Could you do me a big favour and travel with me so you could point out the way?'

'Certainly,' said the farmhand, climbing in. 'Just drive straight ahead. You're lucky, mate, sometimes I send fellows like you around the track about three or four times before they offer me a lift!'

A good pig

A farmer walked into a country pub with a three-legged pig on a leash. The barmaid looked at the drover and then at the pig.

'Two beers, please,' ordered the farmer. 'One for me and one for my pig.'

The barmaid was still staring at the pig as she took the order and offered: 'Must be some pig.'

The farmer looked at the pig proudly and said: 'This pig is one in a million and he goes wherever I go.'

'What makes him so special?' inquired the barmaid.

'He saved my son from drowning in the dam; just waded in and dragged the little lad out. Yes, some special pig all right.'

The farmer noticed that the pig had finished his beer, so he ordered another two pints.

'Yes,' the farmer continued, 'then not long after saving my son's life, our house caught fire and the pig raised the alarm and dragged us all clear: saved the whole family. Yes, some special pig all right.'

The barmaid placed the beers on the counter and looked down at the pig. 'Is that how he lost his leg?'

'Nah!' said the farmer as he downed his beer. 'A pig that special — you can't eat him all at once!'

Sandy's sponge cake

Farmer Sandy was always proud of his wife's ability to make a meal out of practically nothing.

'What are we having for afternoon tea?' he asked one fine day.

'Sponge cake, dear,' said Sandy's proud wife. 'I sponged the eggs off Mrs Doughty, the flour off Mrs O'Toole and the milk off Mrs O'Malley.'

Dad's permission

The young shearer bolted into the church, holding his shears in one hand and his girlfriend in the other. He was sweating like a pig and could hardly be understood, he was babbling so much.

'Help!' he managed to scream. 'We want to get married right now.'

The priest attempted to be priestly and serene but the young man would have none of that.

'We want a marriage ceremony right now!' he blurted out.

The priest said: 'Now, there are certain obligations and routines associated with the holy ceremony of marriage.'

The shearer was becoming increasingly frustrated and belted out: 'Be blowed with your rules — we want to be married right now!'

'For one thing,' continued the priest, 'you must have consent from the young girl's father.'

'Be blowed!' bellowed the young man, gesturing towards the window. 'See that old bloke out there with the shotgun? That's her father and he consents!'

Car went the old way home

Peter Lalor

There's an old journalist who, like many in his trade, was fond of keeping the ink in his blood balanced with booze. Now Jack, as we'll call him, was prone to all-night sessions and tended to get rather muddled.

One night he headed home before sunrise and was obviously sober enough to find his car. (These were the days when that was proof enough of your ability to drive.)

Anyway, Jack got home safely enough, parked the car in

the driveway, somehow made his way inside and upstairs to bed beside his dearly beloved and promptly began to snore away like he hadn't a trouble in the world.

At least, that's the way he tells it.

Early next morning he rolled over, almost killing his wife with his beery breath, opened one bloodshot eye and thought, 'Hang on a minute . . . something's not right here.'

Poor Jack had woken up next to his first wife and somewhere in an adjacent suburb the second one was waiting in a very cranky mood.

'Bloody car went the old way home,' he told us later.

We believed him, but we're not sure if wife number two did.

Visiting the big smoke

There was this bloke who came from the backblocks and he hits the big smoke, parking his ute outside a pub where he knows his mate's sister works.

He walks in and orders a beer and starts up a conversation with the girl.

They get talking and he pumps her for some information on what to do in the city.

She tells him about a couple of good restaurants and clubs and the like, but he seems nervous about going out by himself.

He then asks her to come out with him, but she's a city chick and he's a real bushie and she doesn't want to be seen out with him so she says no.

The bloke has obviously misread the girl.

Then he says, 'Listen, how about coming out with me tonight? I'll shout you dinner and the like and because it's been such a good year on the farm I'll give you $200 for your time.'

She doesn't want to, but thinks she could do with the money and so they go out and have a pretty good time, but she makes it clear that he'd better not get any fancy ideas.

The bloke then says that he's desperate for some, having spent so long on the farm that even the sheep have begun to look cute. He offers to chip in $300 for her time.

The girl has had a few and could do with the money so she figures why not, so they go back to her place and do it.

Afterwards she asks where exactly he's from and is amazed to find he's from the same country town as her brother.

'Wait until I tell him I met you,' she says.

'Yeah,' says the bloke. 'And make sure you tell him I gave you the $500 he owed ya.'

A bit of slap and tickle

Two mates were out on the turps having a pretty good night. They'd known each other since school days and even though one was university educated and the other was barely literate, they got on pretty well.

The smart guy says he'd like to go out and maybe have a bit of slap and tickle.

'Good,' says the slower one. 'I know this bloody great club where you go in, have a couple of beers on the house, then go upstairs with whoever's arrived, have a root, go back down, have a couple more beers until somebody else arrives, then you go upstairs and have another root and so on until you've had your fill. Then when ya leave they pay ya.'

'I find that a little hard to believe,' says the smart one. 'Have you been there?'

'Nah, but me sister has,' says the dumb one.

A dying wish

This old geezer's lying on his deathbed, family gathered around and everyone is feeling a bit emotional.

Even his nagging wife is in a good mood.

'You've been a good husband,' she says. 'Is there anything I can get you, love? Any last request?'

'I don't want to be any trouble,' he says.

'Oh, sweetheart,' she replies. 'Everybody deserves

a last wish. You just ask and I'll do my best.'

'Well, I would love one of those beers you put in the back fridge yesterday,' he says.

'Oh my God,' she says. 'Just like you — selfish and thoughtless. Those are for the wake!'

Give me a beer . . .

This drunk walks into a bar and says to the bartender, 'Give me a beer before the shit hits the fan.'

The bartender gives him a drink and walks off.

The drunk calls him over again and says, 'Give me another beer before the shit hits the fan.'

The bartender obliges and this goes on for a while before the bartender says, 'I hope you've got enough money to pay for these.'

'Oops, the shit's hit the fan,' says the drunk.

Chicken farmer
Jack Stafford

A chicken farmer went to a local bar. He sat next to a woman and ordered a glass of champagne.

The woman perked up and said, 'How about that? I just ordered a glass of champagne too!'

'What a coincidence,' the farmer said. 'This is a special day for me, I'm celebrating.'

'This is a special day for me too, I'm also celebrating!' said the woman.

'What a coincidence,' said the farmer. As they clinked glasses he asked, 'What are you celebrating?'

'My husband and I have been trying to have a child, and today my gynaecologist told me that I'm pregnant!'

'What a coincidence,' says the man. 'I'm a chicken farmer and for years all my hens were infertile, but today they're finally laying fertilised eggs.'

'That's great!' says the woman. 'How did your chickens become fertile?'

'I used a different cock,' he replied.

The woman smiled and said, 'What a coincidence'.

The bear and the barmaid

This bear walks into a pub and asks the mean-faced barmaid — a real bar bitch — for a beer.

'Sorry, mate,' she says. 'Don't serve people without shoes on. Bugger off.'

So the bear gets up and walks out but is back in a few minutes with a pair of shoes on. He sits at the table and asks the mean-faced barmaid for a beer.

'Look, you've got shoes on and that's good, but you ain't wearing a shirt so bugger off,' she says.

So the bear goes out and comes back in a tuxedo,

with a top hat and nice shoes, and thinks to himself that this time the mean-faced barmaid can't possibly refuse him service.

'Can I have a beer now?' he says.

'No,' says the barmaid. 'To tell you the truth I can't stand bears.'

So the bear stands up, rips her head off and eats her.

Wiping the blood off his chin he walks up to the manager and says, 'Get me a bloody beer right now!'

'Sorry, mate,' says the manager. 'Can't serve people who take drugs.'

'Never taken a drug in my life,' says the frustrated and confused bear.

'Oh yeah?' says the manager. 'What about that barbituate?'

The amazing frog

A drunk walks into a pub and says to the bartender that he wants a beer but he's got no money.

The bloke tells him to bugger off.

'Hang on,' says the drunk. 'What if I show you a trick?'

'Well, it'd better be good,' says the bartender.

'Oh, it's good, in fact it's so good I think you should give me two beers.'

'We'll see,' says the bartender.

So the drunk carefully reaches into his pocket and draws out a green frog and places it on the bar. He then reaches into his other pocket and pulls out a miniature piano which he places in front of the frog.

The bartender is amazed, but even more so when the little critter starts to bang out the hottest jazz tunes he's ever heard.

Sure enough, the bartender shouts the drunk two beers.

When he's finished these, the drunk asks, 'If I can top that will you give me free beer for the rest of the night?'

'If you can top that you can have free beer for the rest of the week,' says the bartender, thinking that the pub will be packed with people coming to see the amazing jazz-playing frog.

The drunk smiles to himself and reaches into his pocket and pulls out a lady rat in a slinky dress. The rat leaps from his hand, leans against the piano and sings along.

The bartender is blown away and keeps his word. While the drunk drinks, the rat and frog entertain customers and the pub is packed every night.

On the last night of their deal a theatrical agent walks in and cannot believe what he sees. He immediately offers the drunk $1000 for the frog and the rat.

'Nah, forget it,' says the drunk.

The agent then says he'll give $1000 for the rat alone.

'You're on,' says the drunk.

The agent takes the rat and leaves, but the bartender is furious. 'You just broke up a million-dollar duet for a lousy $1000!' he yells.

'Don't worry about it,' says the drunk. 'The frog's a ventriloquist.'